Twelve military heroes.
Twelve indomitable heroines.
One UNIFORMLY HOT! miniseries.

Don't miss a story in Harlequin Blaze's first
12-book continuity series, featuring irresistible
soldiers from all branches of the armed forces.

First up are those sexy men of the U.S. Army...

THE REBEL
by Rhonda Nelson
January 2011

BREAKING THE RULES
by Tawny Weber
February 2011

IN THE LINE OF FIRE
by Jennifer LaBrecque
March 2011

Uniformly Hot!
The Few. The Proud. The Sexy as Hell.

Blaze™

Dear Reader,

Ahh, Valentine's Day. Hearts and flowers, candlelight and romance. I absolutely love the month of February! Even more fun is adding a hunky military hero to the mix. My own real-life hero is ex-military, so I have a special place in my heart for soldiers and the amazing sacrifices they make for us. So I was really excited to be able to write a Uniformly Hot! story featuring an army hero.

Breaking the Rules is all about control. My heroine, Sophia, finally has control of her life and doesn't intend to lose it again. Max, my hero, has never let a little thing like rules get in the way of what he wants.

Putting these two together made for instant sparks. And where there are sparks, fire's sure to follow.

I wish you a very happy Valentine's Day.

Tawny Weber

P.S. If you're on the web, please drop by my website at www.TawnyWeber.com. I'd love to hear from you.

Tawny Weber

BREAKING THE RULES

HARLEQUIN®

TORONTO • NEW YORK • LONDON
AMSTERDAM • PARIS • SYDNEY • HAMBURG
STOCKHOLM • ATHENS • TOKYO • MILAN • MADRID
PRAGUE • WARSAW • BUDAPEST • AUCKLAND

Recycling programs
for this product may
not exist in your area.

ISBN-13: 978-0-373-79596-3

BREAKING THE RULES

www.eHarlequin.com

Printed in U.S.A.

ABOUT THE AUTHOR

Tawny Weber is usually found dreaming up stories in her California home, surrounded by dogs, cats and kids. When she's not writing hot, spicy stories for the Harlequin Blaze line, she's shopping for the perfect pair of shoes or drooling over Johnny Depp pictures (when her husband isn't looking, of course). Come by and visit her on the web at www.tawnyweber.com.

Books by Tawny Weber

HARLEQUIN BLAZE

324—DOUBLE DARE
372—DOES SHE DARE?
418—RISQUÉ BUSINESS
462—COMING ON STRONG
468—GOING DOWN HARD
492—FEELS LIKE THE FIRST TIME
513—BLAZING BEDTIME STORIES, VOLUME III
     "You Have to Kiss a Lot of Frogs..."
564—RIDING THE WAVES

Don't miss any of our special offers. Write to us at the following address for information on our newest releases.

Harlequin Reader Service
U.S.: 3010 Walden Ave., P.O. Box 1325, Buffalo, NY 14269
Canadian: P.O. Box 609, Fort Erie, Ont. L2A 5X3

To Specialist, James Ramirez.
My very own hero. I couldn't do it without you.

Prologue

SERGEANT FIRST CLASS Maximilian St. James, EOD squad leader, stood at attention at the foot of the hospital bed. Next to him stood the general, also standing ramrod straight. The blistering Afghanistan sun shone through the army medical center window. The sharp scent of antiseptic filled the air.

Specialist Rico Santiago, his leg in traction, returned the general's salute, waiting until the man glanced away before winking at Max.

His face impassive, Max saluted the general and waited for the return salute. As soon as the ranking officer stepped aside for him to pin the Purple Heart on Rico's pajama top, Max rolled his eyes at the look of heroic suffering on his buddy's face.

"Good work, gentlemen," the general concluded, dismissing them both.

Only when the man moved away did Max let himself grin. He tapped Rico's cast and arched his brow as if to say, "Told you so."

"I'd have been fine if you'd presented it," Rico muttered, but Max could tell the guy was seriously proud to have been pinned by a four-star general.

"You deserved a little pomp," Max claimed. He'd made sure his man got it, and had pushed to have Rico brought to the joint theater hospital instead of the closer units. Now, shoulders tense from being at constant attention, Max wished for just a second that they'd stuck with a more low-key hospital.

It had nothing to do with being nervous in the presence of brass. Max had cut his baby teeth on brass.

He'd never had one of his men hospitalized before, though.

He was handling it fine. It wasn't as if he wanted to wince at the sight of the cuts and bruises on Rico's face. The guy's leg all trussed up, with pulleys and contraptions wrapped around it, didn't make his gut clench.

He didn't feel ill whenever he closed his eyes and flashed back to the paralyzing terror of watching the RPG, or rocket-propelled grenade, hit the ground. The dust and flying dirt had made it impossible to see how bad Rico had been hit. For a heartbeat, he'd frozen when the dust cleared and he saw his man lying there on the ground.

Yep, he was handling it all just fine.

Rico was a smart guy, though.

"Dude, quit feeling guilty. It wasn't your fault."

"It was my call to go in and defuse that bomb," Max muttered, giving in to the need to chill by dropping into the chair next to the bed.

"You didn't know we'd be ambushed."

Max shrugged. It should have been a simple bomb detonation. Intel hadn't offered any insurgent warnings. The village had been peaceful with early morning quiet. Standard bomb disarming operation, just like any other day.

Max had assessed the situation and made the call to go in.

It'd been a bad call.

"That grim look on your face is messing up my hero moment here," Rico joked.

"You look pretty in your new jewelry," Max joked, flicking

a finger over the commendation on Rico's chest. "Still, I feel bad leaving you lying here."

"Dude, you'd be going home whether I was busted up or not. Quit being all mama hen and enjoy your leave."

Max smirked, always amused at the hokey folky sayings coming out of a big, macho bruiser like Rico. The man was right, though. Max was due to go stateside in twenty-four hours. It was coming up to the anniversary of his father's death, so whenever possible he took leave to be with his mom on that day.

"But you know…" Rico said, his smile dimming.

Max lost the smirk.

"If you don't mind?"

"Sure, buddy. Anything."

"You're going back to the Bay area, yeah?"

"Yeah." There had been a St. James of *the* St. Jameses on Nob Hill as far back as the 1800s. Sure, the house had been rebuilt after the 1906 earthquake, but the snobbery of the family hadn't changed a bit.

Which meant that while he'd have preferred to spend his month-long leave knocking back tequila with a half dozen bikini-clad hotties on a beach somewhere, that wasn't gonna happen.

Unless orders prevented it, he was expected to spend Februarys at home. Max had learned the rules at his mother's knee. As he'd grown older, he'd learned which ones mattered, which could be ignored and how to bend them all to work in his favor.

"A little favor?"

From the look on Rico's face, a combination of a sheepish grin and the look he got before he pulled one of his notorious pranks, Max figured he'd better hear this standing. He rose slowly, preparing.

"My sister is right outside San Francisco. I told you that, right?" He waited for Max's nod. "She's a peach. A real sweetheart. But she's swimming in the deep end right now, totally out of her element."

Max stood at parade rest, listening to Rico extol the virtues of his little sister, the recently widowed sweet innocent.

"So if you could check on her, I'd appreciate it."

"Just stop in and check on her?" That didn't sound dangerous.

"Well, maybe make sure she's got a handle on her business?"

"Check on her and her business?" Max crossed his arms, eyeing Rico's cast and wondering just how hurt he really was.

"And, you know, make sure any guys sniffing around are worthy."

"Check on her, her business and the men in her life?"

Rico winked. "If you want, you can shovel out the guys. Sophia, she's gorgeous. A real sweetheart. You're gonna love her."

Eyes narrowing, Max rocked back on his heels. "Playing cupid, Santiago?"

"Cupid? Hell, no," Rico said, laughing.

Max relaxed.

"Dude, you take one look at my little sister and you're gonna fall so hard and fast, that flying baby's gonna get whiplash before he can let off a single arrow." Rico levered himself up with difficulty, then slapped Max on the arm. "The two of you? Perfect. Absolutely perfect for each other."

"That bomb rocked your brain? You know I'm not gonna romance your sister. It's against the rules."

"What rules?"

"All the rules. The 'don't date your buddy's sister' rules. The 'don't get seriously involved when you're serving on a dangerous tour overseas' rules. The 'soldiers make lousy husbands' rules." Max arched a brow. "You weren't suggesting I go home and just fool around with your sister, were you?"

Rico moved so fast that the metal bed ground against the cement floor as his traction pulley trapped him in place.

"See, rules." Max nodded, pleased his point was made so easily. "I'll check on your little sister, Santiago. But that's it. Nothing's gonna happen."

1

SIS: IT'S CRAZY HERE. Hot, ugly, intense. My kinda place. Still, I miss home. The pictures you sent of the seal pups in Yerba Buena made me smile. But who was that chick with the pink hair? Did her T-shirt really say Blow Me? What kind of people are you running with? You'd better be careful. You know there are jerks out there who'd take advantage of your money, right? Don't trust people unless one of *mis hermanos* checks them out first, okay? Speaking of, I've got a buddy stopping by. He's a good guy and helped me out of a tight spot. He promised to check up on you. Treat him nice. He's the kind of guy you should be thinking about, okay? A stand-up guy with full pockets and real integrity. Think about it.

Love ya, Rico.

Holy cow, Rico was matchmaking from a battle zone. Her brother was certifiable. Sophia Castillo didn't know whether to laugh or cry. A typical reaction when dealing with her family.

She wasn't sure which was worse, though. That he thought he could check up on her? Or the idea that he'd found some guy who had… How'd he put it? Full pockets? As if she'd have the slightest interest in dating at this point in her life, let alone care what was in some guy's pants. So typical, given that none of the men in her family thought she was capable of taking care of herself.

Sophia smiled anyway, though. Even if he was an over-protective, meddling busybody, she was proud of her brother. Bad boy Rico Santiago had finally found his path in life. A member of EOD, the U.S. Army's bomb disposal unit, he was halfway through his 365-day tour in Afghanistan. Risking his life, defending his country. And still bossing his little sister around.

Trying to boss her around, Sophia corrected as the phone rang.

"Esprit de l'Art," she answered, as always loving the sound of the art gallery's name rolling off her tongue.

"Sophia?"

Recognizing her lawyer's voice, Sophia closed her eyes and said a little prayer, then replied, "Olivia, hello. I hope you have some good news for me?"

"Is no news good news?" the other woman asked.

Sophia winced. If Olivia was trying to make jokes, the morning's settlement negotiation hadn't gone well.

"She wouldn't budge?" Even though she'd known it was a long shot, Sophia's stomach still sank into the toes of her sassy red heels. She'd have dropped her head on her desk and let it bounce a few times, but she figured with her luck she'd damage the desk. And she couldn't afford to replace it.

"I'm sorry. Ms. Castillo's lawyer stood firm on their demands. They want you to release all claims to your late husband's estate. They're not willing to negotiate."

It'd been eight months since Sophia's husband of four years had died of a heart attack. The abrupt loss had been a shock. But the reality was, she'd spent the year before he'd died mourning the loss of the man she'd loved after she'd finally realized the charming hero she'd idealistically married only existed in her imagination.

Nineteen years her senior, Joseph Castillo had swept her off her feet. He'd been wealthy, intellectual and polished. Everything Sophia had dreamed about as a poor little girl growing up in a huge family of bossy brothers and a father too busy supporting all of them to pay much notice to his youngest child.

The first year of her marriage had been a fairy tale. Joseph had been wonderful. He'd even bought the gallery she'd loved since childhood for her as a wedding gift. Indulgent and sweet, he'd treated her like a princess. And she'd done everything she could to be worthy of her charming prince. It'd been in their second year of marriage that things had gotten rocky.

To this day, she didn't know if it was because she'd started feeling comfortable enough to start asserting her normal independence, something she'd sidelined in the uniqueness of being taken care of, or if it was Joseph's waning attention as the novelty of his new bride faded. Probably a combination of the two. But things subtly changed. So subtly it'd taken Sophia three years to see the deliberate erosion of her confidence. A master of passive-aggressive power plays, Joseph had wanted her to remain the naively devoted worshiper he'd married and he'd done everything he could to keep her there.

In the end, Sophia had barely recognized herself under the layers of silk, diamonds and obedience.

And she definitely hadn't recognized the man she'd married.

"So what next?" she asked her lawyer, dreading the answer but needing to know. Never again was she going to hide away and hope things would just get better. She'd learned the hard way that sitting with her eyes scrunched closed and her fingers crossed was only good for wrinkles and hand cramps.

"You want it all, she wants it all. So next, we go to trial," Olivia said briskly, as if Sophia having the intimate details of her life publically smeared in court wasn't anything to stress about. "We have an excellent chance of walking away with everything. Joseph's will clearly stated that eighty percent of his estate was to go to you. Despite your stepdaughter's claim that you were going to file for divorce and in so filing, would void the prenup, you didn't actually take any legal steps. Intention isn't fact."

As usual, the thought of divorce sent a feeling of failure washing over Sophia. She'd been brought up to believe that marriage was forever. Despite her family's oh-so-vocal doubts—or maybe because of them—she'd been determined, even when things started to fall apart, to have that idyllic forever.

Part of her had even hoped that the shock of suggesting they end their marriage would somehow push them into fixing things.

Apparently, she'd still been a little naive. But not any longer. Now she had priorities. And priority number one was her gallery.

"What about the money? Can't I access any of my bank accounts? I've been living on what Esprit brings in for the past six months. And given the mess Joseph created last year, it's not bringing in much."

"The joint accounts are all frozen. I've requested an audience with Judge Langley to negotiate. Ms. Castillo refused arbitration, so I might be able to use that as a leverage to get at least a portion of the money released."

Sophia wasn't surprised that her stepdaughter had refused arbitration. Lynn was bitter. Younger than Sophia by only a couple of years, she'd been raised by her mother and taught young to hate everything her father stood for. Except, apparently, his money.

"I need access to my funds if I'm going to keep this business going, Olivia. We have to figure something out. The gallery has a show scheduled next week. It has to be a success."

For so many reasons. Her ego, for one. Years of subtle put-downs and the slow shredding of her confidence, for another. The process had been methodical and clever. Before she'd realized it, she was distanced from her family, cut off from her friends. Her entire world revolved around Joseph.

His opinions. His approval. His guidance.

Her dress was too short. Her lipstick too bright. Her opinions too loud.

And the gallery he'd given her as a wedding gift? She looked around her office, letting the warmth of the space ward away the chills this conversation and her memories were bringing. He'd never let her actually run the gallery. Yes, it was in her name. But he'd thought she should take management classes. Then he'd figured she needed to travel more, see other galleries. He'd explained that she'd learn through watching. So even though she'd technically owned the gallery for four years, until last summer the sum total of her contribution had been choosing hors d'oeuvres for shows and looking pretty.

And she'd sat quietly by while he slowly and surely undermined the gallery, too. She had to turn the business back around. She and the gallery—they were both going to regain their former glory.

She glanced at the pile of bills mocking her from her in-box and sighed. Somehow.

"Olivia, this show's success is vital," Sophia insisted. Actually, she insisted pretty loudly. Not quite at the top of her lungs, but you couldn't say she wasn't passionate about how much she needed this show to work out. Sophia clenched the phone in her fist and took a deep breath, then modulated her tone. "You have to push harder. I don't understand how she can control everything like this. The will clearly stated what was mine and what was Lynn's. How come the judge is giving her this much power?"

Olivia's sigh was so loud, Sophia was surprised it didn't ruffle her hair through the phone.

"Sophia, I'm sorry. Between Ms. Castillo's witness list and documentation, she was able to present a strong enough case that the judge has to consider it."

"In other words, Judge Langley is listening to gossip and rumors."

The rumors that Sophia was a promiscuous money-hungry tramp had started four months ago. If they were to be believed, it was her fault, for everything from the gallery's shift in focus from classy photography to erotic art, to the resulting financial challenges, to Joseph's receding hairline.

"You realize Lynn's probably the one who started those stupid rumors, right?" Sophia pointed out, her fingers tapping in irritation on her spotless desk blotter. "Who else would care what the gallery is showing or how I run it?"

"Regardless of who started the rumors, you need to be aware of the talk and make sure you rise above it. Prove it false. Continue with your plan to restore the gallery to its former focus on photography instead of the erotic art your husband preferred to show. Behave, keep your nose clean, all that stuff. If you do, we'll be fine. Just stay focused and keep a positive attitude."

At this point, Sophia did let her head drop to her desk as she continued to listen to Olivia reiterate again all the ways she should behave before saying goodbye.

It was all she could do not to slam the phone down. God, she was sick of people telling her how to behave. What to do and how to do it. And always, every freaking time, it was supposedly for her own good.

Because, what? She only did things for her own bad?

When did she get to lead her own life? Call her own shots?

"Now, dammit," she said aloud. "It's my life and I have a plan. I'm the one in charge now."

Maybe talking to herself wasn't a part of that plan, but she was considering it a work in progress.

She clicked her mouse, opening a brightly colored goal board on her computer screen. She'd spent the past year reading every self-help book she could find. She searched her soul, delved into her psyche, tiptoed around her inner shadow. And she'd decided that the true path to happiness was through control. Her taking control of her own life, that is.

And now her brother was trying to get her to go out with one of his buddies? Sophia pursed her lips, and even though she knew she was only torturing herself, she clicked open her picture file.

Her mouse went unerringly to the photo Rico had sent her about six months ago. She'd looked at it so often, it was a good thing it was on the computer screen instead of paper, or she'd have worn out the edges. With a click, a group of men filled her screen. Rico's bomb disposal squad. There was her brother in the center, his arms draped over two other guys while another stood just off to the side.

He was dressed the same as the others, a tan T-shirt and fatigues. But he stood out as if he were wearing a tux. Maybe it was his position, a part of the group yet distanced. Or a sign of authority, since he seemed to be in command.

Some men were pure fantasy material. And this guy, Sophia decided with a deep sigh, was a prime example of a U.S. Armed Forces soldier at its finest. A testosterone-loaded weapon in human form. This guy exuded an air of confident sexuality that was so strong in a photograph, Sophia was pretty sure it'd melt her into a puddle of lust if she ever saw him in the flesh. From the curling tips of his damp, dark hair, over the sculpted muscles lovingly covered in the soft tan T-shirt to the hard thighs in khaki fatigues, he was all male.

All sexy, intense, controlled male.

He looked like the kind of guy who knew how to make sex

amazing. The kind who not only put a woman's needs first, but realized them before she did. A man who'd make her feel incredibly wanted.

Desirable, powerful and feminine. Sophia's breath quickened as she imagined his hands. They'd be strong. Hard, yet gentle as he caressed her. He'd explore her body, sending her into a mind-numbing spiral of sexual delight she'd only dreamt of.

Just like she was dreaming now. Sophia's breath shortened, her body tight and taut at the images dancing through her mind.

Realizing she'd done it again, brought herself to the edge of an orgasm fantasizing about a guy she'd probably never meet, who for all she knew was happily married with five kids, she gave a breathless laugh.

He was definitely not the kind of guy Rico would send with instructions to check up on his little sister.

"Yo, Soph," called a voice from down the hall.

Sophia's fingers fumbled, sending the mouse sliding across her desk before she caught it. A quick click closed the file, and its hunky contents.

Her cheeks burning, Sophia lifted her chin and quickly pushed away from the desk and hurried from her office so Gina wouldn't come in. Her little fantasy had been so hot, she was sure there was a cloud of sexual energy floating above her computer.

"Yo, Gina," she answered, smoothing her skirt as she headed toward the back of the storage room. "Did that shipment of frames come in?"

"Yep. That and a few other things."

That tone, with its underlayer of naughty glee, made Sophia frown. "What things?"

"Oh, some this, some that and a really huge…"

When Sophia reached the far side of the storeroom where

they kept shipping supplies and the deliveries were made, her jaw dropped.

"You've got to be kidding."

"The shippers thought they were doing us a favor by uncrating it since it's so heavy. I was watching the floor, so I didn't have a chance to stop them before they took off." Delighted horror filled Gina Mayes's voice. "Isn't it great?"

Sophia couldn't tear her eyes off the mind-bogglingly huge spectacle to spare her assistant a look.

"I've never seen a penis *that* big. It's insane. What am I supposed to do with it?" she mused with a frown, wandering a circle around the statue for a better look. "I mean, sure, it's pretty. Long, hard and smooth. But really…isn't it proof positive that you can have at least four feet too much of a good thing?"

Tilting her head to one side, her dark hair sweeping across her cheek, Sophia tried to figure out why someone would want to create, let alone buy, such phallic glory. She had no clue.

"Men and chocolate, you can't ever have too much when they're good." Gina grinned from the other side of the erect member, her eyes sparkling behind rhinestone encrusted cat's-eye glasses and below a thick brush of magenta bangs. "And this sucker is definitely bigger than the one I got up close and personal with last night."

"Haven't you heard? It's not the size that counts," Sophia quipped, tongue in cheek. "It's how you use it."

"You just know a man made that up." Gina dismissed her words with a flick of her pink feather duster. "Women know size definitely matters. Even in art."

She might have been married four years, held a master's in fine art and owned a gallery that, up until two months ago, specialized in the erotic. But Sophia didn't have enough experience with men to offer more than a weak smile.

There was no arguing that size was a factor with *this* phallic fantasy. Standing at a solid four and a half feet, fully erect, the polished white-veined marble gleamed in the pale morning light shining through the window. It was going to be a total pain in the ass to return.

"Why do people send their work without checking first? I sent out a notice three months ago that we wouldn't be accepting any more erotic pieces. I made it clear we were shifting focus to photography. Not—" she waved her hand again at the huge penis "—this kind of thing. Erotic art is all well and good, but we're not showing it anymore."

Which was a shame, really. Yes, her plan was to return the gallery's focus to photography, as it had been from its inception until Joseph had decided to stir things up a few years back. But damn, that erotic stuff made a lot of money. It'd be worth polishing a four-and-a-half foot penis for a few months if it'd pay some bills.

Behave, Olivia's reminder rang in her head.

"We'll recrate it and call the shippers," Sophia decided with a sigh, scanning the artist's shipping manifest for an email address. "I'll contact this Mita Andress and let her know we're returning her…penis."

"Andress?" Gina asked. "She called last week, wanting to be included in the upcoming show, but I said her work wouldn't fit this exhibit. Pretty ballsy of her to ignore that. Maybe she thought you'd be so wowed, you'd overlook the topic, so to speak." Gina tucked her feather duster into the back of her wide studded leather belt and wrapped her arms around the marble member to tests its weight.

"I might need a little help," she grunted, stepping back to glare at the large piece as if it'd suddenly made a dirty joke and personally offended her. "Maybe Mita didn't ignore you. Maybe this is another one of Lynn's rotten pranks."

Sophia pursed her lips. The other woman had definitely made it her mission since her father's death to create as much trouble in Sophia's life as possible.

But sending a marble penis?

"Maybe," she acknowledged. "But it's just as likely a mistake."

Unable to help herself, Sophia grabbed her ever-present SLR camera out of the loose pocket of her skirt and stepped back to frame the shot. As always, the viewfinder was magic for her. Her objectivity filter. Through it, she saw what was, instead of what she wanted to see.

She let her mind clear, letting the image fill her head instead. White marble against the pitted paneling of the storage room walls. Gina's face grinning under the pink fringe of her bangs, her torn T-shirt and leather a sharp contrast against the smooth, elegant curves of the sculpture.

All she needed was five seconds to frame and snap the shot for her to put Gina's suggestion to rest. There was too much pride, even love, carved into the marble for it to be a prank.

"I'm sure the artist thought we'd love the sculpture and want to include her in the show next week," she decided as she lowered the camera.

"You just like to think the best of people," Gina accused, as if that was a bad thing.

"Not the best," Sophia demurred. She glanced at the photos lining the back hall, studies of light and dark. "I just see the reality."

"Well, obviously some people don't like the new reality," Gina said with a shrug as she gathered the wood, a can of nails and a hammer to start building a new crate. "I wonder how many more people will send us random body art without a contract, wanting to be included in next week's show."

"I guess I should be grateful someone wants to be included," Sophia muttered, holding the long wooden plank so Gina could hammer the L-bracket in place.

Sophia was sure her decision was right, but the lack of enthusiasm from the public, the artists and the photographers was disheartening. It was almost enough to make her doubt her ability to regain Esprit's previous glory.

Not for the first time, she cursed her late husband. He'd taken one of the top photographic art galleries in the San Francisco Bay area and changed its specialty to erotica.

To this day, Sophia didn't know if Joseph's obsession with sexually focused art was homage to the genre, or if it was a crutch for his own lack of talent in that arena.

"What about that von Schilling guy who wanted to show here?" Gina asked as she started building the next crate wall.

Sophia looked past the crate at the photos, barely visible in the showroom. She'd love to have an artist of von Schilling's caliber showing here. But...

"No. He's amazing, a legend, really. But he specializes in nudes. If I show him, it keeps me stuck in the same rut Joseph created." And would lend more weight to Lynn's accusations that Sophia was some kind of sex-obsessed pervert who would run first the gallery, then the rest of the Castillo estate, into the ground. "He'd be incredible, but I need someone else. A totally different direction."

Seeing that Gina had a handle on the construction of the rest of the crate, Sophia stepped away.

"You could put your own photos in the show," Gina muttered between swings of her hammer.

Pretending she hadn't heard the words over the hammering, Sophia wandered over to the door. Her gaze skimmed the short hallway, focusing instead on the main showroom with its glossy wide-planked floors and beveled glass windows. Prisms of light danced softly, the damaging rays weaving a pattern on the floor but not touching the photographs displayed on the walls.

Her photos, in a show.

It'd be the most amazing thing in the world. Her stomach jittered at the idea, a thrill of excitement shivering down her spine at the idea of being in one.

But she knew what she saw when she looked through the

viewfinder at herself. The truth. She was a lover of art, but not brave enough to be an artist. She didn't have the guts to bare her soul through her work.

What she did have, though, was the gallery. Esprit could be her expression of art. She'd spent years apprenticing, so to speak, at Joseph's side. He'd insisted on dangling the gallery like a gold-plated carrot, his last means of controlling his wife once she'd grown a spine.

Right up until he'd had a heart attack on the ninth hole. A familiar mix of sorrow, guilt and a few dregs of anger roiled together in Sophia's stomach.

She started when Gina patted her arm. She'd been so lost in thought, she hadn't noticed the hammer's silence.

"Soph," Gina said, the look on her face making it clear she had a clue where Sophia's mind had wandered. "You okay?"

"I feel fine," Sophia lied. "I just have to get through this month. Get the show set up, start selling art again. That's my priority."

"My priority is sending this magnificent member back to its maker. But I need your help," Gina wiggled her eyebrows, the light glinting off the stainless hoop on the left one. "I'll seal the last wall of the crate after we shove this sucker inside."

"Pushing penises," Sophia snickered with a shake of her head. "Pathetic."

"Admit it," Gina said, her words barely discernible through her giggles. "You'll miss this kind of thing once the gallery is on the straight and narrow."

"Hmm, let me think. A chance to reclaim prestige, acclaim and worldwide admiration? Or the notoriety of being the proud displayer of the world's largest hard-on? Such a choice."

She didn't add that the constant focus on sex was like nails on a chalkboard to her since she wasn't getting any. Torture akin to sending a dieter to work at a Hershey factory.

She joined Gina next to the statue, watching the tiny woman wrap her arms around the marble. She couldn't even reach one hand to the other, the thing was so wide.

"Yum," Gina said, her face pressed against the penis. "On three?"

Sophia kicked off her twice reheeled red patent pumps and hitched up her pencil skirt so she could bend at the knees. Wrapping her arms around the slick, cool stone, she sucked in a breath and, when Gina said, "Now," lifted.

Holy crap, the thing weighed a ton. They couldn't budge it.

"God," she grunted, releasing one arm from the penis to rub her tailbone. "I think I broke my ass."

"This sucker gives new meaning to the term *rock-hard*. Who knew an erection could weigh more than a horse?" No longer amused, Gina scowled at the monstrosity.

"Can I help you, ladies?" The voice was male, it was laughing and it was coming from directly behind her.

Stiffening, Sophia felt the blood drain from her face.

Did anything say professional like two women wrapped around a preposterously proportioned penis?

Could this get any more humiliating? With a quick wince, Sophia pushed her dark hair off her face and, hoping for the best, straightened the collar of her ruffled poet's blouse before turning around.

It only took two seconds for her blood to heat. For her heart to race. Breath catching in her chest, she stared.

It was him. Her fantasy guy. The sexy soldier from Rico's picture. And he was even better live and in person. Cut military-short, his mahogany hair glinted with hints of red. Laughter danced in his deeply, intense melt-her-heart brown eyes as they met hers.

Sophia wet her suddenly parched lips and tried to catch

her breath. His gaze shifted from amusement to masculine appreciation, the look making her stomach jitter. The man was pure, three-dimensional nirvana. The long sleeves of his blue pin-striped button-down shirt couldn't disguise his wide shoulders, his muscled biceps.

He was a dream come to life. And maybe—she pressed her hand against her stomach—just maybe she wasn't ready to try and handle dreams in real life. They were so much safer in pictures.

It was like getting hit with a sexual force field. Towering a good four inches over her five-foot-ten-in-heels self, he exuded power. Charisma. Pure sexual energy.

"Can I have you—I mean, help you?"

2

TWO WOMEN IN A DIMLY lit room wrapped around an erection that'd do King Kong proud? Struggling against the urge to laugh, Maximilian St. James stepped farther into the store-room for a better look. He wasn't sure what amused him more—the gorgeous blushing brunette's stammers or the scenario itself.

She was stunning. Golden skin that looked like silk over sharp cheekbones, a high forehead and perfect nose. Her lips were full and lush, making him think of deep, wet kisses. He looked into eyes as pale as her hair was dark, watching confusion, embarrassment and what his ego swore looked like lust stare back at him.

A giggle behind the brunette snagged his attention. He squinted at the sight of the other woman. She was...funky? Was that the right term? A cross between a rainbow-hued Goth princess and a very edgy pixie.

Quite the contrast to the dusky beauty staring at him as if he'd just dropped from outer space. His gaze moved past the women to the huge marble cock they'd been hugging.

Shouldn't they be naked? Maybe chanting or something? Was he a pervert for wishing the brunette, at least, had been?

"Am I interrupting?"

At a narrow-eyed look from the taller woman, the pixie choked back her laugh.

Strong women were so damned sexy.

"We were just…" She trailed off, glancing at the statue. Wrinkling her nose, she just shrugged.

He couldn't stop his lips from twitching, but he did manage to hold back his laughter.

Obviously not as constrained, the pixie snorted. At an arch look from her boss, she excused herself to make a phone call, tossing one last naughty giggle over her shoulder as she left the room.

"I saw you just…" He let the words trail off the way hers had. His lips twitched again. "The offer to help is still open. It looks like you could use a strong back."

A faint wash of color swept over her cheeks. She shifted her stance, stepping away from the statue and crossing her arms in a way that accented her curves beneath her loose jacket. His mouth stopped twitching and started drooling.

It was the first time in weeks that he'd felt something other than bone-deep exhaustion or soul-wearying stress pressing down on his shoulders. Maybe it was the year in the desert. Maybe jet lag after the flight into SFO from Afghanistan. Or maybe she was simply the most stunning woman he'd ever seen.

Despite his exhaustion, Max had been dreading this trip home. If he'd had his way, he'd have spent his month's leave in Europe. In Hawaii. Hell, he'd have stayed in the Middle East if he'd had a choice. But now that he'd met Sophia, he was thinking he should be a little more grateful for family obligations and his promise to Rico.

"I'm Sergeant Maximilian St. James," he said, striding forward to offer his hand. Her slender fingers disappeared in his wide palm. "Your brother is Specialist Santiago, correct? He asked me to stop by."

Her scent, a rich, spicy floral, wrapped around him like

an embrace. Delicious. He breathed deeply and smiled. He didn't know what caused the slight tremor in her fingers. She could be intimidated by his size or be feeling an awareness similar to the one surging through his own system.

Discipline was as much a part of his DNA as his skeletal system. Max might be burned out, but he still knew how to maintain control. At least, on the surface. Beneath, though, he felt as if he'd just been rocked by an exploding bomb at the touch of her slender fingers in his.

"Sophia Castillo?" he asked when she continued to stare at him with those sky-blue eyes, looking like she was absorbing his very essence.

"Yes," she finally said, her voice husky. She cleared her throat and appeared to pull herself together, then offered a proprietor-of-the-gallery-type smile. Friendly but not too familiar. He bet that look sold many a… His eyes went to the statue. Well, whatever she sold in this place. "I'm Sophia Castillo."

"Didn't Rico warn you I'd be stopping by?" He'd figured Rico, in typical big brother matchmaking fashion, had exaggerated his little sister's need for someone to look out for her. He'd gone on and on about how she was all alone now. How she'd never run her own life, let alone the business she'd been left by her late husband. He'd made her sound like a twelve-year-old dropped in NYC with a bus pass and a teddy bear.

Rico's hard sell had put Max on red alert. Guilt and obligation meant he couldn't ignore Rico's request to check on Sophia. But he could avoid his buddy's little romance game. He'd labeled this a simple mission. Get in, do his duty, get out. Or in civilian terms, stop by, say hi, make sure she was handling Rico's news okay, then hit the door.

But now? Judging from the dazed look in her eyes, maybe she could use a little help. And if it gave him an excuse to put off seeing his family for a few minutes, or even hours, so be it.

"Rico mentioned someone might, um, might visit. And I recognize you from your…from a picture Rico sent." Another wave of heat, this time for reasons he didn't understand, washed over her cheeks. "You're in his squadron, aren't you?"

"Squad leader," Max acknowledged, noting the resemblance between his specialist and the woman in front of him. Her hair was a glorious black, falling in long waves over her shoulders and giving her the look of a Spanish princess. Slashing cheekbones, a wide mouth and strongly arched brows all defined a strong face. In contrast, her eyes were a cool sky blue, strikingly Anglo against her Latino features.

As if she just realized it was still there, she slid her hand out of his, then took a quick step backward. She ran her tongue over her full lower lip, glanced at the statue and then back at him. She appeared clueless as what to do next.

Maybe Rico was right. Maybe she really did need someone to look out for her.

"Well, thank you for coming by," she said with a semblance of a smile. "I'd love to show you around but, well, as you can see, I'm a little busy at the moment."

They both looked at the dick. Sophia squared her shoulders.

Max frowned.

"Rico just emailed you today?"

"Yes. Or, at least I just got it today. Sometimes his emails take a while to get through."

"And he said…?"

Brow furrowed, she bit her lip and gave him a long, considering look. Her gaze dropped, for just a second, to where his hands rested in his pants pockets—or maybe a little at the center of the pockets, his ego goaded. Then she gave a tiny shake of the head and told him, "He just said someone from his squad would be stopping by."

"That's it?"

She hesitated.

"He also said you'd helped him out of a tight spot. Knowing Rico, I figure he borrowed money or got in trouble with a local girl's brothers. Our dad always said Rico rolls through life like a bowling ball."

Instead of returning her smile, Max didn't move a muscle. His insides froze. The last time he'd felt like this, he'd been staring down the barrel of an enemy's gun. She didn't know?

In the space of his next breath, he analyzed all available options, mentally cursed his luck and decided to go with a soft-sell version of the truth.

"Rico's fine," he said first.

She frowned.

"He did have a little trouble, but it's all taken care of. He's catching up on a little rest and giving some nurses a bad time."

"Nurses?" Her olive complexion paled as her breath hitched. She clenched her hands and then unclenched them. As if she'd grabbed on to the fear and was letting it go before it overwhelmed her. "He's hurt?"

"He's—"

"Don't tell me he's fine again," she snapped. She didn't look helpless now. Then with a show of control he had to admire, she shook her head, took another deep breath and asked in a calmer tone, "Please. Tell me what happened to Rico."

It was her control, rather than her distress, that had Max stepping forward to offer comfort. It was like stepping from the shadows into a warm puddle of sunlight.

"He injured his leg on a mission." He said it brutally fast, knowing that news like this was better given all at once. "We were heading in to neutralize an explosive in a heavily populated area and there was an ambush. He caught some shrapnel in his leg."

As she blinked back tears, her pale eyes studied him closely. "And?"

He didn't move a muscle, but his insides winced. Wasn't she supposed to be helpless and a little clueless?

"Sergeant? What aren't you telling me?"

"I've given you the pertinent details," he said briskly, automatically falling into command mode. Considering his years of military training, his Nob Hill matriarch of a mother and a father who'd been a three-star general, he could pull on "uptight and reserved" like a second skin. "He was on a mission, he was hurt. He's recuperating and will regain full use of his leg."

And all Max had to do was close his eyes and he could see Rico—his tent mate, the guy he played poker with and shared middle-of-the-night terrors—torn and broken. Pale and dead-looking, with blood pouring from his leg and rocks and debris covering his body. His friend. The man serving under him, who'd followed his orders. His responsibility.

He took a step away from Sophia as if he were stepping away from the memories.

"Was that the tight spot you helped him out of?" she asked, her voice tight, as if she were trying to keep tears from falling.

"I neutralized the insurgent responsible while the others on the squad contained the rest of the dissidents."

"You saved my brother?" Her breath shuddered. Then she stepped toward him, laying her palm on his chest as if touching him would ensure his words were the truth. Max's heartbeat increased, just a beat, at her touch.

God, no. He stiffened in horror that she'd cast him as a savior when he knew damned well if it hadn't been for him, Rico wouldn't have been hurt. Max was shaking his head before she finished asking. "We were just doing our jobs. Both Rico and I. Nobody was playing hero."

"He said you helped him out of a tight spot. He wouldn't have said that if he didn't think it was a big deal."

"It was my job," Max insisted through gritted teeth. Just like it'd been his job to send Rico in the first place. Max's gut constricted, a single drop of sweat making a familiar trail down his spine.

It wasn't his fault. Rationally, he knew that. It was his job to give the orders. Nobody could have anticipated the mission going sour. Rico didn't blame him. The squad didn't blame him. Logic dictated that he shouldn't cast blame, either.

That didn't mean they all weren't wrong.

He glanced down at the long, slender fingers heating his skin through the thin fabric of his shirt. Then he looked into her worry-filled eyes, the lush black fringe of her lashes damp with unshed tears.

Max wanted her to be a little friendlier. But he wasn't willing to use his job, her brother or the hellish realities of war to make it happen. He'd stick with charm, thank you very much. Then he'd know he'd actually deserved the affection he planned on earning.

Affection, he reminded himself, that would fly in the face of the friendship rules he'd reminded Rico of.

Which meant he'd have to step carefully. Bending rules was okay. Breaking them? Something to consider very, very carefully. Not that Max had ever found a woman who had tempted him enough for him to actually go that far. But there was something about the sweet Sophia...

"Look, Rico's fine," Max assured her, putting as much compassion into his tone as he could find. He knew he should step away, disconnect, but he couldn't bring himself to. Not when she was so warm. "He'll spend a few days in the hospital, then a week of R&R. If there were any thanks necessary, he's already offered them. And in return, I promised him a favor."

Max hadn't meant to mention that. It must be the worry

shadowing her eyes that'd wormed it out of him. She'd be a hell of an interrogator. All she'd need to do was look sweet and vulnerable and guys would be tripping over their words to get her to smile.

Then that worry shifted. First she frowned, just a little, then she narrowed her eyes. Just like that, they went from liquid to ice. Max was good at reading people. But as he watched Sophia's face get tight and distant, he couldn't tell if it was irritation or embarrassment. But what did she have to be embarrassed about?

"A favor?" she questioned softly.

"Friends do friends favors," he defended, not sure why he suddenly wished for his bomb suit. "Why's that a problem?"

"No problem. Unless, of course, that favor had anything to do with me."

Smart woman.

"He just asked me to look in on you. Check and see how things were going."

"Rico thinks I need a babysitter? That's it?"

Max's smile spread slowly. "What else could it be?"

"Nothing. Absolutely nothing," she muttered as she stepped back, putting some distance between them.

Immediately missing her scent, Max closed the distance again.

Her eyes narrowed. She took another step back. He took another step forward.

Her eyes narrowed. This time, he knew it was irritation.

"I appreciate the visit. But as you can see, I'm hardly the little girl Rico considers me. I'm fine. I don't need a babysitter."

"I don't mind," Max said with a grin. "Rico would do the same if I had a sister."

"Ha. Rico can't be trusted. If you introduced him to any

woman, as long as she was of age, he wouldn't think twice about seducing her."

Was that like permission? Max's grin grew so wide, it hurt his cheeks.

Sophia blushed. Then she drew her shoulders back and gave an aristocratic tilt of her chin.

"If you're just getting back to the States, I'm sure you have things you want to do," she said, her desire for his departure as blatant as the big ole penis she was standing in front of. "I appreciate you stopping by and bringing the news about Rico."

She offered Max a distant smile. The kind you gave a stranger on the street. Brief and impersonal. He wasn't sure why it annoyed him so much. He'd wanted her to treat him naturally, not to coat their exchange with misplaced gratitude. She obviously thought this was a courtesy visit and was happy to keep it at that.

But he wasn't.

He wanted more.

"Soph?" They both turned, Max squinting a little at the sight of Sophia's assistant. She wasn't any less shocking the second time around. "I talked to the shippers. They'll be here in ten minutes to pick up the crate."

"Ten...?" Sophia puffed out a breath, her gaze bouncing from the other woman to the huge erection and then landing on Max. For just a second, she looked softer. Vulnerable.

Then she pulled herself together and offered her hand to Max to shake goodbye. He took her slender, warm fingers in his and held on. Her eyes widened in a look of heated curiosity. He'd seen that look often enough to know his interest was reciprocated.

Then she pulled her fingers away and stepped back. Apparently *reciprocated* didn't mean *welcomed*.

"I guess I have a penis to pack," Sophia joked. Then she winced and gave him a rueful look. "Or, well, you know what

I mean. I really do appreciate you stopping by and reassuring me in person that Rico's okay."

Max hadn't made Sergeant First Class in the U.S. Armed Forces by being slow, though.

"I'll crate this up for you," he offered with a manly smile. He hoped it didn't show his distaste at handling any penis other than his own. "Then we can get a drink and talk about that favor to Rico."

"I appreciate the offer, but Gina and I can handle things here," she insisted.

Max wasn't sure if she kept protesting out of pride, stubbornness or some weird need to have the statue to herself. But they were all stupid reasons, so he went with what he always did in cases like this. Exactly what he wanted.

Stepping around her, he eyed the polished mahogany base against the floor of the crate. He grabbed the three-sided box and gave it a shake to test for sturdiness. Satisfied, he nodded and turned back to the women.

"This should work fine."

"Of course it'll work fine. Believe it or not, this isn't the first phallic statue we've dealt with," Sophia told him, sounding a little affronted.

The magenta-haired Goth-pixie snickered.

"We'll be fine, but thanks," Sophia continued.

"Why won't you take my help? I'm here and offering myself," he insisted. Then, unable to resist, he added, "C'mon. You know you need me."

Sophia opened her mouth, then pressed her lips tight. A hint of color warmed her cheeks. That look of interest was back, warming her blue eyes. Her gaze traveled the length of his body with a familiarity that made more than his shoulders snap to attention.

And yet, she still refused. What was with this woman?

"Thanks, but—"

"Sophia, we really could use his help. The delivery guy

was laughing when he called. He said it took three of them to uncrate it." The girl's gaze danced behind her cat's-eye frames as she swept her eyes over Max. Her eyes lingered, heated, and then she grinned as she inspected various body parts. He had to stop himself from covering his goods. "He definitely looks...big enough to handle the job."

Max had defused bombs that made him less nervous than the look on the magenta-haired woman's face. Then he noticed the same speculation in Sophia's eyes. As if she were measuring, weighing and wondering just how big he was. Her gaze slid over his body, appreciation warming the sky-blue depths as she assessed what he had to offer.

Max was pretty sure flexing his biceps would be classified as pathetic. He ordered the rest of his body to refrain from flexing, as well. Not that the rest of his body was listening. All its attention was focused on Sophia. The scent of her, the warmth that seemed to radiate from her smile. The curves that made his mouth water as if he was three-days-dehydrated.

"Okay, sure. I guess we do need help," Sophia finally said, making a show of looking at the clock. "Let's get to it, then."

She and Gina ranged on either side of the statue, Gina going into a wrestler's squat. Sophia stepped out of her high heels again before hitching up the slender lines of her skirt so her knees were free of fabric.

Max's body went as hard as freaking marble at the sight.

Knees, for God's sake. He'd been in the desert way too long.

"All we need to do is slide it up to the edge of the crate," she told him. Her hands curved over the gleaming white marble in a smooth caress. He didn't think she was aware that she was running one hand up, then down, as she pushed with the other to test the weight of the statue. "Once it's past the edge, we can wiggle it onto the base until it's all the way in."

Max stared. He could actually feel the heated path his

blood took on its way south to his shorts. He had a vision of her in that same position, but wrapped around him. Because God knew, the way she was making him feel, he was pretty sure his current erection could compete with that man-size sucker.

"Why don't you two hang on," he suggested, his tone a little strangled. "Let me try this myself first."

Gina stepped back right away, obviously glad to let him do the heavy lifting.

"We can help," Sophia stubbornly insisted. "After all, it's actually our job."

Oh, no. The way he felt right now, watching her keep on handling that penis—hell, any penis—was going to make him cry like a baby. Right after he exploded.

Desperate to get it over with, he stepped behind her, gently slid his hands under hers to release her grip, then grasped either side of her waist. He lifted. For a tall woman, she didn't weigh a damned thing. And luckily she was too shocked to do more than stiffen and gasp when he moved her aside.

"Hey…" Her words trailed off as she watched him unbutton his cuffs. He shoved his sleeves up to his elbow so he could get a good grip on the marble.

Max approached the dick the way he'd approach a ticking bomb—with a great deal of respect, trepidation and determination. His arms couldn't span its girth. For a brief second, he wondered who the hell had posed for this sucker. Then, needing that thought as far from his brain as possible, he started silently reciting detonation codes.

He tilted the statue back toward him, then pushed until it met the edge of the crate. He angled it just so, then lifted. He squinted as the room flashed for a second, then, figuring it was just exertion, grunted and pushed the monster onto the crate bottom.

Almost there.

His muscles trembled as the marble slipped a little under

his sweaty hands. God, if the guys saw him now, he'd never live this down. That was all the motivation he needed to give it one last shove.

And done.

Not even winded, Max stepped back, dusted his hands together and gave the ladies a triumphant smile. It faded a little when he saw the camera Sophia was tucking into her pocket.

She hadn't, had she?

He narrowed his eyes, trying to read her face. Pure innocence.

Oh, yeah, she had.

He'd just have to get her to delete it. The St. James men were used to getting their way. All he had to do was decide on a strategy. In this situation, he figured a little charming persuasion should do the trick.

"Easy enough," he said, referring to both the crating and the upcoming photo deletion mission.

"Thanks so much. I really do appreciate both the news of Rico, and your help."

Gina grabbed a hammer and a few more boards. Giving him her own smile of gratitude, she went to work packing up the crate.

"Don't you think you owe me at least a drink? As a thank-you?"

She frowned, taking her time sliding her shoes back on as if his request was of monumental concern.

Max wasn't sure whether to be insulted or intrigued by her obvious reluctance to spend any more time with him.

"Sure. We can get a drink. As a thank-you for your help, and to toast my brother," she said finally. "I don't want to take up too much of your time, though. I'm sure you have quite a few better things to do on leave than check up on your squad mate's sister, Sergeant."

"Sophia, we just spent five sweaty minutes together,

wrapped around a mammoth erection," he pointed out, giving her his warmest smile. She blinked twice and sucked in a quick little breath.

"We're practically intimate now. So you might as well call me Max." He loved the way she looked, all flushed and flustered. He wondered if that's how she looked when she made love. "And don't forget to bring that camera."

3

SERGEANT FIRST CLASS Hottie St. James.

He was first-class, all right.

Oh, God. What were the chances that the guy whose photo she'd been dedicating orgasms to would show up in her gallery just when she'd sworn off relationships? Fate, or Rico, had a wicked sense of humor.

Skirting around the temptation to brush against the hard length of his body as Max held open the gallery door, Sophia averted her eyes and held back her sigh. This was crazy. She felt like a schoolgirl whose *Teen Beat* poster had just come to life.

The man was absolutely gorgeous. Even sexier in person than in the photo she'd spent months fantasizing over. He oozed charisma like a gooey caramel-filled chocolate oozed deliciousness.

And she was starving.

For the first time in her life, she wanted to strip a man naked and nibble her way down his body. She, who'd never stripped off so much as a man's shoes.

Sophia almost tripped off the sidewalk imagining what Max might look like naked. She'd spent four years immersed in sexual images, erotic art and, hell, just today had wrapped herself around a four-foot-tall marble cock. And none of it came anywhere close to heating her up, making her want to play out the *Kama Sutra,* like this guy did.

"Slow down," he said, almost making her jump out of her skin when he put a cautioning hand on her forearm. "Gotta watch for cars."

Baffled, she looked up one side of the empty street, then down the other. Cars?

Before she could ask, a motorcycle came around the corner, speeding past from the opposite direction.

"Or motorcycles," he amended with a knowing smirk.

It was that cocky look that punctured her sexually induced bubble. As if he was not only right, but always right. She almost tripped over her feet again as her mind did a quick replay of the last hour. He'd swept in, taken over and she'd… what? Fallen right back into her old habit of letting someone else take over.

She remembered Rico's email. Deep pockets. So not only was Max bossy and domineering, he was rich. Two strikes, right there. And with the lawsuit and swirling rumors of her promiscuity, she definitely couldn't afford to try for three.

Not even for what promised to be, in her limited and inexperienced opinion, the most incredible, intense, wild sex of her life.

No. This was going to be purely a thank-you-and-goodbye drink. She'd be friendly but distant, in a he's-just-her-brother's-friend kind of way. And keep to herself all fantasies about nibbling her way down his chest on her way to paradise.

"Are you sure this isn't too far?" he said as they reached the door of the cantina across the street from the gallery. "We could have sat on that bench there in front of your place and shared a bottle of water."

"Clever," Sophia said, grinning despite her intention to stay aloof. She sailed past him when he held the heavy brass-trimmed door open.

Why couldn't he just be bossy? Did he have to be so freaking cute and charming, too? His picture hadn't said charming, dammit.

Sophia knew that unless a photographer was extremely talented, charisma rarely translated on film. Especially the sergeant's kind. He had a charm that combined clever humor with sexual undercurrents, and that charm promised sensual adventures to anyone willing to hand over control.

Which meant, as usual, Sophia would be missing the sexual satisfaction boat. Because this girl wasn't giving up control ever again.

With that in mind, she called on the hostess skills she'd perfected—the one area Joseph had deemed satisfactory— during her years of marriage.

"This is my treat. A thank-you for all you've done for me and my family," she told him as they stepped into the cool, plant filled foyer of the cantina. "This is a great place. Wonderful ambience, great appetizers and fast service."

"By all means, let's make sure we're served quickly," he agreed, waving his hand to indicate she proceed him. "Dragging out gratitude is such a pain, don't you think?"

A laugh gurgled out before Sophia could control herself. The only thing sexier than those rock-hard biceps he'd shown off when he'd hefted that obscene statue was a wicked sense of humor.

The hostess stepped forward, a pair of gold menus contrasting with her brilliant red blouse and flounced skirt.

"Hi, Carmen. We'd like a table for two," Sophia said after the older woman greeted them.

"Right this way," Carmen invited after giving Max a little leer and then offering Sophia a naughty wink. "I've got the perfect spot."

Oh, no. Her body already in motion, Sophia's feet froze to the floor. She almost fell on her face. The perfect spot. The designated date table.

"Perfect is overrated," she murmured, hurrying to catch up to Carmen. "How about a place by the window instead?"

Carmen frowned, shaking her round, dimpled face. "But the afternoon sun is glaring on that side of the room. The perfect table is shaded. Much more comfortable."

"I like the afternoon sun," Sophia said with a stiff smile, willing the hostess to understand that she didn't want the date table.

"Maybe we could get the drinks to go," Max drawled, obviously getting the message Carmen wasn't. "Avoid these pesky table choices altogether?"

Sophia grinned. Giving up on the unsuccessful subtlety, she tapped Carmen's rounded shoulder and pointed to an empty table that overlooked her gallery. "We'll take that one, okay?"

The hostess's heavy sigh as she seated them spoke volumes. Her inhalation told Sophia just how hot she thought Max was, and her exhalation exclaimed her despair over her friend's poor dating skills.

Sophia gave her own sigh of agreement. Even she couldn't argue that those skills weren't pure crap.

"What can I bring you both?" Carmen asked as they sat on opposite sides of the scarred plank table.

"Whatever dark ale you've got on tap," Max requested.

"Pomegranate margarita, please."

"Mmm-hmm." With that and one last look of frustrated despair for Sophia, she flounced off with a swish of her full red skirt.

A busboy set chips and salsa between them. Sophia nibbled nervously, not sure what to say now. She didn't know how to talk to a man. She knew how to talk to guys, of course. Brothers, fathers, artists. Friends, even.

But sexy men whose photo she'd spent months fantasizing over? Men who confused her, making her want to flirt one second and yell the next? She had to swallow hard to get the fried tortilla past the lump in her throat.

She stared at the tabletop, realizing that she was so totally out of her element here.

"You know," Max drawled after Carmen had set their drinks down and flounced away again, "I don't think I've ever felt so appreciated."

Sophia's fingers clenched the chilly stem of her margarita glass. She lifted her eyes from the frothy red drink to meet Max's dark gaze.

Oh, no. He'd obviously taken her insecurity and nerves as bitchiness. Despite his teasing tone and easy smile, his words cut deep.

"I'm so sorry." Sophia leaned across the table to press her hand to his bare forearm. "You've been nothing but helpful, and I'm being rude. Rico would be shaking his finger in my face if he knew."

Max's laugh lit up his entire face. "He does that to you, too? We rag him about it all the time. Big tough soldier boy, wagging his finger like a nagging granny."

Sophia giggled, her heart softening to hear the affection in his voice for her brother. "He's done it since he was little. We always called him *abuela niño* when he did."

"Granny boy? He must have loved that."

"I do believe that's one of the reasons Rico's so good with his fists," Sophia said with a laugh.

"You said 'we' called him *abuela niño*. Who's 'we'?"

"My older brothers and I. There are seven of us. I'm the youngest, under Rico."

"Seven?" Max's eyes rounded. "Your parents were ambitious."

"It's the only thing my mother ever stood up to my father about. She wanted a little girl and wasn't willing to stop until she had one." Sophia's tone was as bittersweet as her smile.

According to her father, that rare streak of stubbornness had cost her mother her life.

Obviously hearing the underlying pain in her words, Max gave her a searching look, but was gentleman enough not to pry. Instead, he changed the subject. Telling her stories of Rico's funnier mishaps and the practical jokes he'd pulled overseas, he swiftly moved the discussion from pain to laughter. Sophia loved hearing about her rough, tough, kick-ass brother in the words of a man who clearly appreciated Rico's sense of humor, quick temper and fierce pride.

Ten minutes and the contents of her margarita glass later, Sophia had relaxed.

Instead of the aggressive pursuit she'd expected, Max showed gentlemanly restraint with a subtle underlying charm.

"Is it my imagination, or do the figures in that painting look familiar?" he asked as he fished out the last chip from the basket. He offered it to her, and when she shook her head, popped it into his own mouth.

Sophia didn't have to follow his gaze over her shoulder to know what he was referring to. She did have to hide her surprise that he was observant enough to have recognized her and her brothers, though. Especially since the painting was twenty years old.

"No, it's not your imagination," she assured him. "My father used to own this restaurant. When he sold it a few years ago, the new owners asked to keep the decor and art."

He studied the painting, then tossed back the last of his beer. "Dating must have been hell," he decided.

"I beg your pardon?"

"Six older brothers looking out for you? A guy would have to be pretty brave to risk that and ask you out." His words were teasing, but the look he gave her clearly said he was definitely brave enough.

Sophia's stomach tumbled a little. He made her want so much. From him. From herself.

"My brothers were bullies," she confirmed a little breathlessly. "But they're all scattered now and busy with their own lives. These days, nobody vets my dating choices except me."

"Is that so?" The look he gave her was pure flirtation. The giddy, giggly, naughty kind that had her pulling back her shoulders, thrusting out her breasts and fluttering her lashes before she even realized she was responding.

Damn, he was good.

Sophia immediately stopped pulling, thrusting and fluttering.

"But given that I'm not in a dating place in my life," she quickly added, "it doesn't matter. All six of my brothers could be camped out in my gallery watching my every move. They'd be bored to death with the lack of bullying and intimidating opportunities."

"Maybe they'd turn matchmakers instead and find you the perfect guy," he teased, an odd glint in his dark eyes. "Do you think they'd take applications?"

And there it was… Her own personal version of hell. Six over-testosteroned bossy-boys ruining her life. Lurking, judging, taking over. They'd start by telling her how to dress, move on to telling her all the mistakes she was making at the gallery and end with a complete rearrangement of her world.

Her pain must have been evident on her face, because Max suddenly looked stricken.

"Oh, man, I'm sorry," he said quietly, reaching over to warm her hand with his. "That was insensitive of me."

Without thinking, Sophia turned her hand so they were palm to palm. Little tingles of excitement built, swirling from her hand all the way up her arm and down her belly. The palm was an erogenous zone? She was so sexually clueless.

"I forgot that you were recently widowed."

Sophia stared.

Well, shit. Sophia slowly slipped her hand from his. She slid it onto her lap, clenching her fingers together.

She'd forgotten, too.

What was it about Max that made her forget important things?

In the past, she'd have fallen back on her tried-and-true litmus test. She'd have taken his picture. Photos were windows to the soul, showing the real person. No matter how they piled on the mundane disguises, a well-shot photo let her see the true person. Their inner being, so to speak.

It'd been photographs that'd helped her see that her father, a man who ruled his house with an iron fist, was a pussycat inside. Photos had let her see the worry lines carved into his forehead, the responsibility pressing down on his shoulders after he'd lost his wife. The pride in his dark eyes and the love in his rare smile.

Seeing that had made his controlling attitude easier for Sophia to understand. Whereas photos of her late husband had showed an entirely different story. An affable surface, with a streak of mean domination underneath. A warning to watch out for bossy men with charming surfaces.

Like the one sitting across from her.

Her fingers itched for her camera. A waste of time, though. A photo would only confirm what she already knew. The man was pure eye candy, wrapped in a layer of sexual charisma. And underneath all that temptation? He was an alpha leader to the core. The kind of man who issued orders without thought and always expected to be obeyed.

Sophia had never considered herself a sensual woman. She'd even wondered if Joseph was right, that she was a little frigid.

But now? Yes, the sight of Max was a major turn-on. The man was seriously sexy, massively gorgeous. But that was aesthetics. She'd spent years in school viewing equally stunning models, men who turned heads by just walking into a room. But she'd never felt this tug of desire deep in her belly. A spark, a sexual one, that told her that he'd make her feel things she'd never even imagined.

Hands shaking a little at the concept, Sophia lifted her glass, hoping to find a few more comforting drops of tequila.

Was she so insecure in her own strength and independence that she couldn't enjoy a sexy man's company unless he was a wimp who wouldn't threaten her control?

"I'd love to take your picture someday," she blurted out. Her eyes grew round, jumping from his to her empty glass. She hadn't meant to say that aloud.

"More than the one you shot of me back in the gallery?" he teased.

Sophia wrinkled her nose in a self-deprecating little wince. "You saw that, huh?"

"Why'd you think I told you to bring the camera?"

He reached over and made a little gimme motion with his fingers. She laughed, then pulled the camera from her pocket, toggled it to the view option and, after a quick look, pressed her lips together to keep from snorting.

She didn't release the camera, but turned the view screen so he could see the shot of himself in a half squat, hugging the huge white penis.

Max stared, his dark eyes round in horror.

She waited for the explosion.

He burst into laughter.

Heat swirled low in her belly, making her thighs quiver. God, she wanted him.

"Nice job," he complimented, taking the camera to get a closer look. Sophia's fingers itched to grab it back, so she curled them into her palms. The camera was like another limb. She hated being without it.

"I don't know art that well, but you perfectly captured not

just the weight of that marble, but how freaked out I felt. So is that what you show at your gallery? Blackmail shots?"

Sophia laughed as he leaned back in the chair, draping one arm along the back of the seat next to him.

"I doubt there are enough blackmail shots out there to pull together much of a show," she said thoughtfully. "But that would be fun, wouldn't it? It'd probably be a bigger draw than my upcoming romance show."

"Romance?"

Sophia hesitated, so used to her ideas for the gallery being dismissed as soon as she offered them. But Max looked genuinely interested, so she took a deep breath and leaned her elbows on the table.

"Romantic photos, to be precise. Esprit has been…" What? Sinking in depravity? Selling out for the quick buck? Peddling sex instead of art? She went with, "Floundering in its focus for the past few years. I'm hoping this show, my first show since taking over, will get us back on track. We're shifting away from all other formats to focus exclusively on photography."

"Hence turning away the big dick?"

She grinned. "Exactly. Despite Esprit's reputation and history, my late husband thought he'd make more money if he shifted focus to erotic art."

"Reputation and history? Esprit de l'Art," he mused. "I know that name for some reason. Something besides Rico talking about it, I mean."

"Did you grow up locally?"

"San Francisco, born and bred," he confirmed.

"Then you probably have heard of the gallery. Not only was it declared a historic site seventy years ago, as it was one of the buildings that survived the 1906 fire, but it's also made the news for the shows and dignitaries it's drawn over the years. The building itself is owned by the Historical Guild."

"Isn't Esprit one of the most exclusive galleries in Northern California?"

"Yes," she said enthusiastically, thrilled that he'd recognized it. "The gallery started out featuring only California artists and subjects. Pretty soon artists were moving to California for a chance to show here. Until four years ago, its main focus was photography."

"I remember it now," he said. Then he smiled with quick charm. "Are you thinking of showing your own work?"

"No," she said quickly. "My work isn't showworthy."

"But you want to take my picture?" Unspoken, but clear on his face was the question "Why?" She didn't know how to answer him. She didn't think admitting he turned her on and she needed to see him objectively before she gave herself permission to strip naked and straddle his body was an appropriate response.

Especially since it was insane. A woman trying to reclaim—hell, to claim for the first time—control of her life didn't grab the first opportunity to climb all over a man who'd proved in the first five minutes to be just as domineering as her father, her brothers and her ex-husband.

"It's not a big deal," she demurred. The picture wouldn't matter. Because this wasn't going anywhere. She might not be able to control her reaction to the man, but she could damn well control whether she chased after him like a lust-starved groupie.

MAX WASN'T STUPID. THAT offer to take his picture had been an opening. A very brief one, too, since it looked like it'd closed already. Too bad. He'd pose with a whole forest of penises if it meant she'd give him another one of those dreamy wasn't-he-the-best-hero-in-the-world? looks.

"Another drink?" the waitress offered on her way to the bar.

He saw the automatic no on Sophia's lips. Then her pale

eyes met his and she hesitated. Taking advantage of that mil-lisecond, he tilted his head, winked, then offered, "I have some recent pictures of Rico you might enjoy."

"You play dirty," she murmured with a rueful laugh.

"I play to win." The words came easily to his lips, said millions of times over in his life. But now, instead of filling him with inspiration, it just made him tired.

He'd been raised to win. To win and to take care of re-sponsibilities. But lately, he'd felt as if he'd gone a round with a bomb and lost. Maybe it was burnout. Maybe it was the scare of seeing Rico hurt. Maybe it was the letter listing all the things his mother needed him to do when he got home. Either way, he'd been feeling a little rough.

At least, he had until Sophia. She was a refreshing treat. Gorgeous and sweet, with just a hint of sass.

And like any treat, it'd be better if he drew out the enjoy-ment. So he gave the waitress a smile and, pointing his finger, indicated another round. He shifted his focus back to Sophia and let his smile warm and widen.

"If you look that pensive over a drink, are you going to give yourself wrinkles if I order a plate of appetizers?" Max asked.

"Appetizers?" Sophia frowned.

"It's not that I'm ignoring your hurry-up-and-drink man-date," he assured her. "I'm just hungry. Other than airplane food, I haven't eaten in half a day. Are you going to deny me the pleasure of real, U.S.-made food?"

"You've got an answer for everything, don't you?"

There was something in her voice again. Something cau-tious and a little chilly. But Max could tell from the reluctant amusement dancing in her eyes that he'd be getting his plate of nachos.

Sophia twisted in her seat and waved her hand to get some attention. The move made her ruffled blouse gape. Just enough to give Max a peek at the golden glory of her full breast and a hint of white lace.

His mouth went dry. The waitress arrived with their drinks and, after a quick look of inquiry, Sophia ordered the large nacho platter. Max could still see her breasts in his mind, though. He imagined sliding his fingers, just the tips, over those lush mounds. Tracing the pristine white lace where it met the silky contrast of her skin. He gulped his beer.

"You said you had pictures of Rico," she reminded him when the waitress brought the food.

Rico.

Hell.

Frowning, Max pulled out his cell phone and punched up the photo application. He kept his eyes on the pictures of his squad, the guys still on the front line depending on him. He bit into a cheese-and-shredded-beef-covered chip and told himself to get over the inappropriate lust.

Rule Number One: You don't go after a buddy's sister, even if he gives you permission, unless you're serious. And serious about sex doesn't count. That's quickly followed by rule number, well, probably Rule Number Seven or Eight if he was being honest. Rule Number Eight, then. Don't hit on vulnerable women.

Sophia being Rico's recently widowed sister made her off-limits according to both rules.

But…

Max had never met a rule he wasn't tempted to challenge.

"Tell me more about the photos you take," he invited, giving her his most charming smile. "Are they nudes?"

Her eye roll didn't quite disguise her amusement.

"Forget I said anything," she instructed. She poked her finger at the camera still on the table between them. Then after briefly sucking on her lower lip and trying to drive him insane, she pulled it toward her and said, "I'll go ahead and get rid of that shot."

Max's hand covered hers before he was aware he'd moved. "Let me get this straight. Not only are you rescinding your offer to take my picture, you're now going to delete the only shot you do have of me?"

Her eyes went smoky blue, sparked by a sudden fire that had flared somewhere inside. Max's body responded to that look as if she'd used it to strip him naked and write dirty suggestions on his bare skin. Instant, flaming passion.

"Why don't we take your camera and a pitcher of those margaritas to go and see what kind of scenarios we can shoot," he said, keeping his tone light, even though he was serious as hell.

Her eyes rounded. The blue depths held a hint of sexual curiosity that made his ego sing. But if he was reading her correctly, there was worry and just a little fear there, too.

God, what was wrong with him? Max felt like a bigger dick than the one they'd crated earlier. He was getting all turned on and seeing sexual innuendo in her look that he knew she didn't intend.

Rico had described her as innocent, despite her marriage. Sweet. And here Max was, horny as hell, ready and willing to take advantage of that sweet innocence.

Whether it was his suggestion or if she'd actually read his thoughts, she slipped her hand and the camera away.

"Like I said, I'm not a professional," she told him. "And while this was lovely and I really enjoyed hearing about Rico, I really need to get back to the gallery."

Taking the rejection in gentlemanly stride, Max nodded. He ignored her insistence on paying the tab, left the waitress a couple of bills and tried to help Sophia from her seat. He was so distracted trying to sort out why he felt so disappointed that he barely noticed her irritation.

He didn't want this to end yet.

All the way across the street, he fought the urge to slip his guiding hand from the small of her back to the curve of her slender waist.

Like any good soldier, he strategized on his feet. He marshaled his arguments, backup plans and contingencies in the sixty seconds it took them to reach the sidewalk in front of the gallery.

He had too much respect for her to use the lonely-soldier-home-on-leave ploy, but he wouldn't hesitate to pull out the Rico card. Yes, he'd love nothing better than to take her away to some secluded rose-covered cottage for a weekend of romance. But he'd settle for dinner. What nonthreatening restaurant should he suggest? The trick would be to keep it light. No scaring her off by hitting hard and horny.

Then she stumbled. His hand shot out, grabbing her around the waist and pulling her tight against his body. She gave a little cry of surprise.

"What're you doing?" she demanded, her words breathless, her eyes huge.

"Saving you from falling." And pressing his luck.

"I don't need…" Her words trailed off as realized how close they were. So close her scent filled his senses. Close enough for him to see the faint sprinkle of freckles on her golden skin.

He could see his own desire mirrored in her pale eyes.

To hell with the rules.

Two steps and they'd reached the side of her building. He backed her up against the bricks, bracketing her body between his and the wall.

Max leaned down and took her mouth. Her sweet, tequila-laced gasp reminded him that taking advantage of a woman who'd been drinking was totally out of line.

Then she gave a little shudder, her breasts shimmying against his chest. She reached up, locked her hands behind his neck and between one breath and the next, she was the one taking his mouth. Her kiss was decadently sweet. Soft. Incredible.

Her tongue traced his lower lip, then his upper. She nibbled, she rubbed. She tempted.

She was driving him insane.

Max groaned. His hands slid down her back, smoothed over her hips. Then, unable to resist, he reached around to cup the delicious curves of her ass. Her delighted little groan brought him to his senses. What the hell was he doing?

"Not here," he murmured, pulling away and trying to find his famed control.

"But here feels so good," she protested, her hands tightening on the back of his neck.

"Inside," he insisted, pulling her arms down and taking her hands.

The passion in her eyes dimmed, replaced by insecurity. She lifted her chin, giving him a look that made him feel as if he'd just kicked a kitten and now she was going to hiss and spit.

"Max, I'm sorry," she started. He didn't have to hear the rest to know she was handing him a rejection. And since he didn't want to hear it anyway, Max interrupted.

"Inside," he repeated, pulling her around to the front of the building. That kiss had been hot enough to melt his shorts. If she was going to boot him to the curb after it, he'd rather it wasn't here on the street, with the hostess grinning at them from the cantina across the street.

Not listening to her sputtering protests, he pulled her through the door.

But once they'd stepped into the gallery, his defenses immediately shifted from lust to protection. His senses on full alert, he squared his shoulders and stepped in front of Sophia to shield her with his body.

"Oh, my God," Sophia breathed, either in shock or because she needed support, her trembling hand clutching the back of his shirt.

"What the hell happened here?" he demanded.

4

SOMEONE HAD MADE DESTRUCTION an art form.

Max wasn't an expert, but it looked to him like it totally clashed with the gallery's decor.

The two tall ficus trees that flanked the door had been shoved over, a messy arc of leaves and dirt dulling the gleaming surface of the hardwood floor. One of the blue velvet settees flanking the walls had been upended, its wooden legs covered in shards of glass from any of the half-dozen broken picture frames that'd crashed to the floor behind it.

In the middle of it all was Sophia's assistant, her face almost the same color as her hair.

"I was in the back with the shippers, then uncrating the frame order. I heard something and came out to this..." She looked shocked, waving ineffectively at the scattered glass, tears pouring down her cheeks. "The bell over the door never rang. I don't know..."

"Call the police," Max ordered.

The pixie started bawling and Sophia trembled against his back.

But neither woman moved toward a phone. Max reached into his pocket for his cell phone.

Dead.

Damn. He hadn't charged it. Given that his mother and uncle were the only ones in the country who'd be contacting him, he'd preferred to not make it easy for them.

A quick glance through the showroom didn't net a phone. "Is the phone in your office?"

"Yes," she responded absently, her focus on the mess that'd once been her beautifully pristine showroom. "I need to clean this up."

At that, her assistant hurried out of the room.

"Don't touch anything until the police get here," he instructed

"I can't just leave it like this." He could hear the despair in her words. She finally stepped around him to face the mess. Max instantly missed her warmth.

The pixie returned with a broom. Sophia went to her, hugging the sniffling woman briefly before taking the broom and murmuring a few comforting words.

"I know it wasn't my fault," Gina said tearfully. "But I still feel horrible. I should have been paying better attention after the last time."

"This has happened before?" Max snapped.

Sophia gripped the handle so tight her knuckles were white, but her look was serenely controlled when she glanced back at Max. "This building's had some problems the past few months. A little graffiti, some vandalism. A few harassing phone calls."

Rico was right. She did need protecting.

"You've notified the landlord, right?"

Sophia sucked in a deep breath. He yanked his gaze from the deliciously tempting curves of her breasts. This was the wrong time to be getting turned on.

"Max, I appreciate your help. But I can handle things here."

"What happened before? What did the police do?" he asked, ignoring her.

"They can't do anything," she repeated. She took the broom back from him. "They've been out for the vandalism and the ugly phone calls. All they can do is write a report. There's no evidence, no witnesses, nothing for them to do anything with."

"Right, but they still need to come out. Why don't you check the rest of the gallery, make sure nothing else was damaged. I'll go call the cops." Before she could snap, Max added, "The sooner it's done, the sooner you can sweep up this mess."

SOPHIA WAS PRETTY SURE smacking Max around the head with her broom was illegal. But it was tempting. Still, just like calling the cops, she knew it would be pointless. With a head as hard as his, he probably wouldn't even notice.

Trying to resist the urge, she pulled her gaze from Max's. The only place to look, though, was at the destruction of her showroom. Her stomach shuddered at the sight.

Sophia forced herself to breathe, blinking fast to keep the burning tears from pouring down her cheeks. She had to clean up. She'd be damned if she'd fall apart.

"Fine. You don't want to check the rest of the gallery, can you point me in the direction of a phone?"

"I told you—"

"Soph?" Gina stood in the marble column-flanked doorway, tracks of mascara streaking her pale face. "I called the police."

Sophia had a brief urge to kick something. Why was it that whenever she tried to assert her independence, someone swooped in and undermined her? And always because they thought it was for her own good.

Did she have some freaking neon sign flashing overhead claiming her incompetence? She glanced back at Max, his sleeves rolled up to show strong arms. Arms that'd been wrapped around her ten minutes ago. She let her gaze wander up those arms to his shoulders, broad and strong. They'd felt muscular, hard, solid under her questing fingers. Her eyes rose, tracing his strong neck, a neck she'd held on to while he'd kissed her.

Her eyes locked on his mouth. Heat swirled low in her belly as she relived the pressure of that mouth. The rich taste of him. The power, passionate and needy, he'd ignited in her body. The way he'd made her think that all the fascination with sex, with erotic delights, was actually warranted.

"Can you show me the rest of the gallery?" Max asked Gina. After a quick glance at Sophia for permission, the girl nodded and led him out of the showroom.

Sophia's hands gripped the broom so tightly, she was surprised the handle didn't splinter. God, this was insane. Her stepdaughter was trying to ruin her life. She had a show coming up next week that needed all her focus. And now her gallery was a mess. And all she could think about was how hot Max St. James was.

The guy was obviously just as detrimental to her sanity as he was to her self-control.

And a part of her didn't care. Closing her eyes, she rested her forehead on her hands where they gripped the broomstick. Maybe she should stop reading self-help books on independence and control and start reading about codependence recovery. Was she the kind of woman who said she wanted to be strong, then sabotaged herself?

Before she could consider that too closely, Max returned. "I checked the back, the offices and other showrooms. This is the extent of the destruction."

His gaze traveled over the dirt-and-glass covered floor until it reached the broom in her hands. His eyes made a slow sweep up her legs, over the curve of her hips, and heated as he noted the flat planes of her belly. She sucked in her tummy and said a quick thanks that she'd turned to Pilates to fight her sexual frustration.

Then his eyes rested on her breasts. Heat washed over her, tingling and warming its way through her system. Her nipples beaded against the soft cotton of her bra, making her ache for more than just his eyes on her. She could picture his hands, large and strong. His fingers circling and petting. His mouth, hot and wet. Her breath quickened. Her body fought against itself, a part of her melting while the rest of her went on high alert. She wanted to curl into the pleasure, and didn't want to miss a single second of the experience.

Her gratitude shifted from her Pilates workouts to the broom in her hands, since it was the only thing holding her upright.

And Max was apparently so sexually intuitive, he knew exactly how she felt.

"Sophia?" His words were low, a sensuous thrum that moved through her welcoming body.

"I don't want this," she whispered. Still, as if working independently from her brain, her body leaned toward him. She could almost feel the hard heat of his chest against her aching nipples, welcomed the imagined pressure, hoped it'd ease the aching heaviness.

"Do you want me to talk you into it?" he asked, his words teasing, but his tone making it clear all it'd take was a nod from her and he'd get to work on the convincing.

Wouldn't it be incredible? All she had to do was let him take control and she'd have what was sure to be the best, most incendiary, sex of her life. And she didn't even have to make the choice. She could just stand here, breathing heavily, and let him take that as complicity.

Talk about seductive.

"Don't mean to interrupt, but did one of you call the police?"

It was like taking an ice-cold public shower. Her lust vaporized in a blast of searing embarrassment. She wanted to kick and scream and throw something almost as much as she wanted to give the cop a hug for his timing.

Max looked like he just wanted to scream and throw things, though. Then he blinked and the look of frustration was gone.

"We've had a break-in," Max offered, stating the obvious as he strode forward to shake hands with the officer. "It appears to be confined to this room, but I'm sure you'll want to check the rest of the building."

Still trying to corral her raging libido, Sophia watched Max handle the cops. He identified himself as a concerned bystander, introducing her as the owner with a wave of his hand. Then he and the cop proceeded to ignore her while they discussed the vandalism. A part of her wanted to scurry off to her office, sink into her couch and let him fix it all.

But she couldn't. She wanted independence, which meant handling things like this herself.

"Officer, I'm the one you need to talk to," she said, stepping forward to interrupt them. "Sergeant St. James was just leaving."

"Sergeant?"

And there they went, off on their male bonding bonanza. Sophia spent the next ten minutes feeling like an interloper as she tried to interject answers, only to have the cop ignore her in favor of Max. Finally, she'd had enough.

"Officer, do you have any further questions for me? No? Then I'm sure you have a lot of serving and protecting to do elsewhere. Me," she said with a stiff smile as she jerked a thumb toward her chest, "I have to clean up my gallery, check the photos closer for damage and get them all rematted and reframed. So if you'll both excuse me."

The policeman nodded, apparently so used to rudeness that he didn't even blink at the abrupt dismissal. He started jotting down a few more notes on his report, then pulled out his card to write something on the back of it.

"Sophia—" Judging by the concern etched on his face, Sophia knew Max was the kind of guy who took helping others seriously. So seriously that he was happy to step right in and take over. Which she didn't need.

"Max, it was wonderful to meet you. Thanks so much for letting me know about Rico." She rushed through her words, suddenly realizing that once the cop left, she wouldn't be safe. From herself, that was. So she needed Max out, too.

"Ma'am, here's my card. The case number is on the back, if you need to contact us."

She took the card and risked her body's rebellion by taking Max's arm with the other hand. Smiling, she pulled Max along as she escorted the cop to the door. It took five minutes and all her powers of persuasion and charm to shoo them both out.

"I'll be in touch," Max said, digging in his heels at the threshold. He gave her a long look, then let his gaze slide over to the side of the building where he'd kissed her. "Soon."

Torn between wanting to make him promise and needing to tell him to stay away, Sophia just shook her head and murmured thanks for the drink before shutting and locking the door.

She'd have sagged against it, but she knew he'd see her clearly through the beveled glass. So she set the broom aside and headed down the hallway.

"Mmm-mmm, you'll have a great time jumping his bones," Gina said, following her into the office.

"Not in this lifetime," Sophia shot back, crossing her office to the little refrigerator in the corner and getting a bottle of water. Then she shook two Advil out of the bottle in her desk drawer.

"Why the hell not?" Gina asked, her tone hitting a new high note. "He's freaking hot."

"Hot or not, I'm not dating him."

Gina crossed her arms over her chest, shifted her hip to one side and gave Sophia her patented are-you-insane? look.

"Look, he was appealing while we were munching on cheese-covered tortilla chips. He's a nice guy and a friend of my brother's. But that's it."

"Nice enough that you let him borrow your lipstick, hmm?" Gina arched her brow.

Heat raced up Sophia's cheeks.

"Okay, fine. So I gave in to the urge to taste." And oh, God, he'd tasted so good. So, so good. "But one taste was enough. Will there ever be another? No way. Did you see the way he just took over? This is my gallery and he wouldn't even let me decide when to call the police."

"In his defense, he wasn't the one who called them," Gina said around the thumbnail she was nibbling.

"It doesn't matter who called. What matters is how Max stepped in and took over. The man didn't listen to a word I said."

"He sure looked like he was listening," Gina said. "He hardly ever took his eyes off you."

Sophia had to force herself not to blush like a schoolgirl. He had stared. A lot. He'd made her feel wanted and sexy and special. He'd also made her feel incompetent and frustrated and useless.

"No," she said, as much for herself as for Gina. "He's too bossy. Sexy charm and a gorgeous body aren't enough to make up for the simple fact that dating him would be a disaster."

"It doesn't have to be forever, Sophia," Gina said in exasperation. "You're not required to hand over your spine along with your underpants."

"Easy for you to say," Sophia muttered. Gina was the kind of girl who put her own needs—especially sexual—front and center in everything she did. Sophia didn't know if it was because of or despite that attitude that she and Gina had become such good friends.

Giving in to the multitude of frustrations that'd been her day, she threw herself on the tapestry couch and pulled a pillow comfortingly against her chest.

"I'm saying just date the guy. Have a good time. Enjoy life. Maybe get a little."

Sophia rolled her eyes as if the idea of getting a little, or a lot, with Max didn't make her thighs melt. Even if he hadn't been brother-approved—which would only give Rico all sorts of pro-interfering ideas—he had too much in common with Joseph. Rich, bossy, charming. Three strikes.

"He's a soldier, isn't he?" Gina asked in a suggestive tone.

"What's that got to do with anything?" Sophia gave in to the lure of comfort and kicked off her heels, tucking her feet up. "I'm not checking the size of his weapon."

"Ha ha. What I'm saying is he's home now on leave, right? That means he's only here for a little while. Temporarily."

Sophia wasn't so tired she didn't immediately get Gina's point. Temporary.

Could she put up with Max's bossiness in exchange for his sexy company if she knew their time together was limited?

Or was that just an excuse to let herself visualize them naked together. His body hard and strong, poised over hers while she trailed one hand over his shoulders and the other down the flat planes of his six-pack.

Naked was good. Finding out what all the fuss about sex was would be even better. But Max St. James? That man was purely bad news for a woman searching for independence.

"Just think about it," Gina ordered. "I'm going to clean the showroom, then head home. I'll check the locks on my way out, though."

Sophia waved her friend away and gave herself another minute to pout.

Then, calling herself a whiner, she rose and went to her computer. She moved her mouse and clicked, pulling up her goal board. Yes, a fabulous and gratifying sexual relationship was typed right there in its purple box. Right next to the box labeled vacation in Greece and the one marked meet Wayne Dyer. All of them were in the uncontrollable column. Dreams, wishes, someday possibilities. The only three purple boxes on a goal board filled with yellow boxes. Yellow boxes were career, business, security. Yellow boxes were things she could control. Purple boxes were things she had no control over.

She sighed, dropping her head against the cushioned leather back of her chair.

So what did she focus on here? Control? Or a man who not only made her forget all of her lessons, but was so bossy he made her brothers look like pushovers?

Nope. There was no choice to make. And since her body was used to being denied pleasure, it shouldn't be too difficult to forgo the promise of passion. It was just a matter of control.

Besides, there was no way he was as good as she was imagining.

"HOME SO SOON, MAXIMILIAN?"

"What? No brass band and confetti?" Max returned, stepping around the chilly disapproval of his mother's question at the same time he stepped across the threshold into the world according to St. James.

He handed his duffel bag over to Sterling, the St. James's butler, and returned the man's welcoming smile. He swept his gaze over the opulent foyer, noting that it looked exactly the same as it had a year ago when he'd shipped out. The same as it had ten years ago when he'd graduated high school. The same as it probably had almost three decades ago when his nanny had brought him home from the hospital.

Some things never changed. Speaking of which, he took a deep breath and turned to face the woman standing in the arched dining room doorway.

"Hello, Mother. You look wonderful."

"Do I? It must be the evening light. If you'd bothered to come home directly from the airport, you'd have easily seen all of my worry lines." She didn't step toward him, but did lift her chin so he could kiss her smooth cheek.

"I had some things to take care of." Things that apparently didn't want to be taken care of. Max told himself he'd be crazy to let himself get hurt because he'd been brushed off by a woman he'd only known a few hours. "But I'm home now and you can stop worrying. I'll take care of everything."

"I didn't say I needed anything taken care of, Maximilian. I'm handling my life just fine. I just wish I heard from you more often, even if you only bother to come home once a year."

And yet, it felt as if he'd never left. Max wanted to do an about-face and march right back out the door, then he looked more closely at his mother. She'd aged since he'd last seen her. Tabby St. James's blond hair was still a smooth fall to her chin. As usual, her evening suit was Chanel, her perfume the same and the pearls at her throat and ears heirloom. But there was worry in her dark eyes, a hint of fear and relief as she did a visual inventory. As if she couldn't trust his, or the Army's, assurance that he'd been fine overseas.

It was that look that extinguished Max's ire. She might be the queen of guilt trips, but she did love him. In her way. Since she'd think a hug forward and inappropriate, he laid his hand on her shoulder and gave a light squeeze.

"I had an obligation to attend to," he said, wincing at both the side step and at terming the delicious time he'd spent with Sophia as an obligation. But from the look on her face when he'd left, he was pretty sure she'd use the same term. Or worse. "My cell phone was dead or I'd have called to let you know."

"Well, no matter now." Tabby fluttered her hands in a way that some might take as dismissing the issue, but Max knew it meant she was only shifting it aside for later. "Let's eat before dinner is cold."

And God forbid Tabitha St. James serve anything that was less than perfect. Her dinner rules were etched in granite.

He followed his mother's elegant steps into the dining room, offering the man seated at the head of the table a nod of greeting.

Max took his seat, noting the familiar gleam of his mother's best crystal and china. The food served might change, but the tradition remained the same. He knew the table had been set and waiting since that morning, ready for whenever he arrived. Formality was the rule of thumb for the first meal home. It had been the same when his father was alive.

Max waited until the gazpacho was served before greeting his uncle, the four-star general.

"Sir."

"Sergeant. Eat up, then you can tell me all about your latest adventures."

Yet another tradition. Ever since his father had died nine years back, when the General visited, he sat at the head of the table, taking charge. The man directed the meal like a military campaign. Everyone had a role, with him in charge.

Something Max wouldn't question in the field. But here at his mother's table? He didn't mind stirring things up a little here.

"Not many adventures to share, sir," Max told him, since the ones he knew the General wanted to hear would only give his mom more of those worry lines she liked to complain about.

For the next few minutes, Max shared an upbeat version of his current tour, downplaying the dangers and focusing on the friends and time he spent on base instead of in the field.

"Don't you think it's about time you transfer to a higher profile outfit?" his uncle asked. "I've got connections, some pull with certain people. You can start working your way into a more politically strategic position."

"I prefer to stay with my current assignment, sir. I want to be on the front line doing what I was trained to do. I'm making a difference." Max looked at his soup instead of into his uncle's steely gray eyes and admitted, "What I'm doing matters. One day we save a kid, another a village. The war is ugly. I feel like I'm doing my part to keep it from getting any uglier."

The General leaned back so Sterling could replace his soup with salad, waiting until all the plates had been served before shaking his head.

"You're letting sentiment instead of intellect steer your choices. That's not a good idea, Sergeant."

"They're my choices," Max said without heat. He'd heard different choruses of this same song most of his life. His uncle, just like his father before him, had a specific plan in mind for Max's career. Max wasn't playing by any plans but his own, though.

"Don't be discourteous, Maximilian," his mother said, uttering her first words since they'd sat down to dine. Such was the hierarchy, Max knew. His uncle, like his late father, claimed precedence. If the General hadn't been there, Tabby would have controlled the conversation. As a child, Max had often wondered when his turn would come. Then, when he'd grown older, he'd hoped it never did.

"Darling," his mother continued, "while you're home, I hope you'll find time to socialize. There are many people who'd love to see you again. And I've accepted a number of invitations on your behalf."

"I'm home to help you, Mother. To look over the finances, take the car in for service, make sure the house isn't falling apart," he said, only half teasing. This was his job. Once a year, come home to personally make sure everything was running smoothly. It was how he justified the joy and freedom he felt the rest of the year.

"Your mother's right," the General put in. "Obligations are necessary, of course. But so are building the right connections."

Connections. Both the General and Tabby believed strongly in the power of networking. The most influential people, the correct alliances, the smartest services. Every decision was weighed with an eye for how it'd enhance the St. James name and reputation, from the boarding school Max had been sent to at four to the military school he'd graduated from. His major act of defiance had been to enlist the minute he'd left high school instead of attending West Point.

"We'll see," Max hedged. "Mother's books and the estate take top priority. And I've a number of personal obligations to see to, as well."

He could imagine the look of outrage on Sophia's face if she'd heard him refer to her as an obligation. Hell, he just might tell her so he could enjoy the fireworks. The woman was definitely exciting.

"Don't be silly, darling," Tabby said quickly, as if rushing to stave off an explosion. Since the tension in the room had reached electric proportions, she was probably smart. "I've got Bobby, the gardener's assistant helping me out with all those little jobs, so you'll have plenty of time to socialize."

"You just said you were having problems," the General reminded her tersely. "Over drinks, before Max arrived."

"Well, yes," Tabby said, looking flustered. "But nothing that requires Maximilian's attention. The historical society has an issue with a particular building. We feel the business is too controversial and would like it shut down or moved."

His attention was more on keeping himself from drooling over the rich wine-scented coq au vin Sterling had just set before him than on his mother's comment. His knife and fork were in hand before her words sank in.

"You can do that?" he asked. "Shut down a business because you don't like them?"

"Well, it's not easy, but yes, eventually we can."

Max grimaced. As usual, Tabby didn't take note. Instead she changed topics right back to the list of women she'd lined up for him to date. Dates they both knew Max would avoid. Then her chatter shifted to the upcoming country club winter ball.

That, he wouldn't be able to avoid. Maybe he could convince Sophia to go with him, though. Max recalled the way she'd hustled him out of her gallery and smirked. Right. He was pretty sure she'd just as soon ride naked across the Golden Gate Bridge than date him.

Probably on that marble cock.

5

HER SHORT, APRICOT-TINTED nails tapped an irritated beat on the wood of her desk while Ryan, her insurance agent, droned on over the phone. Sophia stared so hard at her computer screen, her eyes watered and the bright colors of her goal chart bled together.

Every few seconds she made a humming noise to indicate that she was listening.

Five minutes later, she carefully eased the phone from between her ear and her shoulder, gently pressed the Off key and, keeping a pleasant look on her face, swiveled her chair so she could set the phone in its charger.

Across the room, Gina sank deeper into the tapestry couch, chewed off the purple polish on her thumbnail and waited for the explosion.

Sophia pursed her lips as she glanced at the two pages of notes she'd taken during her conversation, then closed her eyes and sucked in a deep breath.

Apparently unable to stand it any longer, Gina asked in a tiny voice, "Are they raising the rates?"

"They're considering it," Sophia acknowledged. "Apparently police reports add to our risk factor."

To say nothing about how they added weight to the ugly

rumors. Olivia had already called this morning to chide Sophia, pointing out that they were supposed to be downplaying the evidence for Lynn, not add to it.

"I shouldn't have called them," Gina said, sounding like she was going to cry. "I just thought…"

"No," Sophia said with a quick shake of her head. "If you hadn't called, Max or I would have."

"I'm sorry."

Sophia shook her head at her assistant, looking so forlorn behind her red and black striped cat's-eye glasses. "Gina, don't worry about it. Seriously. Ryan gave me a list of things I can do to keep the rates from increasing."

"Like?"

"Like…" Sophia stalled for time by looking at the list. She blinked a couple of times to clear her eyes. Most of them were impossible, but Gina didn't have to know that. "Add bars to the front windows. Install cameras and upgrade our security system. Get stronger releases from the artists."

She gave Gina a bright, cheerful smile and flicked her finger at the last item on the list. "And the easiest? Find out who's messing with us and have them arrested. Ryan figures since the graffiti and vandalism have escalated in the past month, it probably has to do with the upcoming show."

"The show?" Gina narrowed heavily lined eyes. "I don't think so. This is personal, if you ask me. Do you think this is all happening because of your money-grubbing slut status?"

"Huh?"

"All those rumors about your competency, about you being a tramp who pushed your husband into focusing on sex statues to make money? They all started after your stepdaughter contested the will, right?"

"Right."

"Now you're changing the focus of the gallery. Eliminating the erotic art it's been known for. You're showing all new

artists. You're trying to bring in a totally different clientele."
Gina talked so fast, her high-pitched words almost tumbled
over themselves on the way out of her mouth. "We both know
that for all Joseph's sex-sells philosophy, the gallery wasn't
doing so well the past couple years. But if you turn it around,
reclaim its former glory, Esprit's going to be huge again. I'll
bet Lynn's furious about that."

Tears blurred Sophia's eyes so fast she didn't even have time
to blink. God, she was tired of this. For eight months she'd
been fighting Lynn for Joseph's estate. She'd struggled with
fear over every damned choice, every freaking decision.

Sniffling, she glanced at her computer screen, her goal
board a blur of colors.

"You're right. She probably is behind it all. But I can't prove
anything. I've told Olivia my suspicions, and she's told the
police. All anyone can do is watch and wait." Sophia clenched
her fists in frustration. Always, it seemed, she was stuck in
the passive role. "Meanwhile, I can't give up. I deserve my
dream, don't I? I'm willing to work for it. To fight for it."

She pushed away from her desk, stepping barefoot toward
the hall where she could see her once again spotlessly beautiful gallery.

"I've wanted this since I was ten. When I helped out at
the cantina, I'd spend my breaks sitting at the table by the
window, wearing my brother's hand-me-downs and watching
the fancy people coming and going through the gallery."

"What was it like? Glamorous? Ritzy? All artsy and bohemian?" Gina asked, anxiety forgotten as she drew her knees
up into story time pose.

"Bohemian?" Sophia laughed, her tears forgotten as she
curled up on the couch next to Gina. "Just how old do you
think I am?"

Gina rolled her eyes and waited.

"It was incredible," Sophia said softly. She stared at the
photos framed on the opposite wall. "The beveled glass win-

dows were like jewels on an elegant lady. In the evening, between the lunch and dinner hours, the sun would hit the brick of the building, turning it the color of a soft rose. It was just so romantic-looking."

She smiled, the memories flooding back. "It was pretty casual during the day, but for shows? Oh, man, it was gorgeous. The women would wear fancy dresses, the men suits. It just screamed class to a girl with dishpan hands and a bowl haircut to match her brothers'."

Gina giggled. With good reason, Sophia knew, since she'd once shared a pitcher of margaritas and childhood pictures with the other woman. She'd been raised by her father and six older brothers; it hadn't been until she'd left for college that she'd learned the finer points of being female. At ten, she'd been just one of the boys.

"My dad used to let me come over once in a while and I'd stare at the photographs. The way they were displayed, the stories they told. I wanted to be a part of this world so badly," Sophia admitted, tracing one finger over the patterned fabric of her sofa. That's why she'd taken up photography. The first time she'd looked through the lens of her dad's old camera, she'd known she'd found her passion. She'd saved for a year to buy her first camera. "I think I saw it as nirvana. A little piece of heaven."

"And you got it, right?" Gina said, sounding unsure.

"In a way. Joseph bought the gallery as a wedding gift. A way for me to have my dream and still keep an eye on my father. This was before he'd sold the cantina."

Sophia remembered how naively thrilled she'd been, believing that Joseph had actually meant that the gallery would be hers.

"So you're going to recreate that world?"

"It's all I ever wanted for the gallery. I mean, c'mon, erotic art? Penises and orgies? That never screamed elegant or classy to me, you know?"

Gina nodded. Sophia had hired her despite Joseph's protests, finding a kindred spirit in the wild younger woman. Gina had been at the gallery for about a year before Joseph had died. She knew firsthand what kind of man he'd been.

"Well, you have to admit that diamond-tipped bust of, well a bust, was pretty elegant."

"Girls with Grills?" Sophia winced, remembering how hard it had been to convince Joseph not to buy it himself. By that time, they'd not only been in separate bedrooms but entirely separate wings of the estate. But still… "Bling does not elegance make."

"I know," Gina gushed. She leaned forward in her best gossip pose, humor glinting in her eyes. "Like the current trend of bedazzling your coochie. Vagazzle. Talk about overkill."

Sophia's laugh gurgled out.

And just like that, all of her stress and anger dissipated. That was one of the things Sophia loved about Gina, her ability to enjoy the absurd in life. And to make Sophia want to do the same.

"Exactly," Sophia agreed enthusiastically, pointing her finger in agreement. "I mean, what's wrong with good old-fashioned girly bits without rhinestones?"

"Nothing, if you ask me," a man's voice offered, laughter lurking behind his words.

Gina jumped so hard, she slid off the couch. Apparently deciding three was a crowd, she stood and hurried out of the room.

Nerves suddenly on full alert, Sophia shivered. All her life, she'd figured lust was the thing of romance novels. Now she found out lust was not only all too real, it could be ignited with just the sound of Max's voice.

Just the man she'd been trying to pretend she didn't want to see. She gave herself five whole seconds—an eternity, in her mind—to gather her control, and to struggle to put her sandals back on. One hand on her stomach to try to calm the horde of horny butterflies zinging around, she sucked in a breath, then opened her eyes.

"Sergeant, I didn't hear you come in." She stood, smoothing her skirt and offering a hand that barely trembled. He looked…delicious. She'd told herself he couldn't be as sexy as she'd thought. That it'd just been the tequila, the upset over the vandalism, that'd skewed her perception.

And then she'd spent all night dreaming about him.

"It's Max, remember?" He took her hand in his, subtly pulling her a little closer. The move doused her passion like a cold shower. The man was such a control freak; he even took over the simple greeting.

"Right." She slipped her hand from his and stepped back. Enough to show she was in control. And almost enough to keep her knees from melting. "I'm surprised to see you again. I thought we said our goodbyes yesterday? Or did you have another message for me from my brother?"

There. She smiled, pleased. That should put him in his place. Which was out of her reach, clearly marked off-limits and dangerous.

"The police suggested that your problems are probably due to a grudge or vendetta. They don't have the personnel to stake out the gallery," he reminded her. Sophia's smile faded. "I went ahead and pulled a few strings. Three of the top private investigative firms in the Bay Area are coming by this afternoon to talk to you and offer bids."

"What? You…? No way…" She was so shocked at his audacity, she couldn't even finish a sentence. She tried to catch her breath, sure that when she could breathe again, the spots would fade from her eyes and she could glare properly.

"You've got to be kidding," she finally sputtered. "What possessed you to presume such a thing? Do the women in your world always expect you to shove them aside so you can take over?"

His friendly look shifted to confusion. She felt bad. She

knew she was taking her own issues out on him. That wasn't fair. He probably didn't mean to be pushy. Here she was jumping all over him—and not in a good way—and he probably thought he was being considerate.

"I wouldn't say I expect women to let me take over," he answered with a puzzled shrug. "At least, no more than the men do. I mean, if I'm the best person for the job, it doesn't matter who steps aside to let me do it, right?"

"Step aside? Best person?" All of her conciliatory intentions flew out the window as his words set fire not only to her issues, but her temper. Before she could grab that control she kept telling herself she wanted, she exploded.

MAX LEANED BACK AGAINST the wall, his eyes narrowed as he watched Sophia rant, her hips swinging with a little Latin flair as she paced the room. She tossed her lush hair, punctuated her accusations with huge arm waves, cussed in both English and Spanish.

She was incredible.

He let her words wash over him, instead letting the delightful view finally calm the churning that'd been making a mess of his gut since the previous night's meal. By dessert, his mother had tried to arrange three dates for him, dumped the company's audit on his shoulders and begged for his help with her little historical society complication.

A complication called Sophia.

If there was one thing he knew, it was that any connection between his mother and a woman he had sexual designs on meant only bad things. Tabby was like the kiss of death to Max's sex life.

A mother's fondest wish, he figured.

"Look," he finally interrupted. "Not that I'm not enjoying the show, but the first guy's going to be here any minute now. Maybe you can yell at me later?"

Sophia stopped pacing so fast he was surprised she didn't

fall off those sexy heels. Strappy sandals today, he noted, in a hot red leather in the exact hue of her toenails. Delicate little toes and smooth arches wrapped in criss-crossing bands. He wanted to slide those shoes off her feet and scatter soft kisses along her delicate ankle. Up her smooth calf. Along the sensitive flesh behind her knee.

He shoved his hands in his pockets, wondering when the hell he'd developed a foot fetish.

"Did you listen to a word I said?" she snapped, the demand in her tone pulling him from his contemplation of how it'd feel to have her toes work their way over his body. "Were you even paying the least bit of attention?"

"Sure," he lied, adding a charming smile to lend weight to his words. "You don't want a P.I. poking into your history or embarrassing you by asking your friends and family nosy questions. Esprit is your business and if you wanted an investigator, you'd hire one yourself. And as for who I think I am, I'm assuming that was rhetorical since we both know I'm the guy your big brother sent to look out for you."

Max's smile slid into a smirk. He couldn't help it. She just looked so cute standing there, her fists on her hips and her mouth working like a fish trying to breathe. After what she'd told him about growing up with her overprotective brothers, he knew brandishing the Rico card was pushing his luck. But hell, he defused bombs for a living. He was used to playing on the edge.

"You're…" She just stared, her hands waving around as if she was trying to grab the right words out of the air.

"A great guy? Yeah," Max said, straightening from the wall and stepping forward until he was a few inches away. Close enough to really appreciate the way anger made her eyes go a deep blue.

And close enough for her to smack him good if he didn't watch his step.

With that in mind, he wiped the grin off his face and

tempered his words as if he were talking to a shock victim. "I'm here to help, okay? I'm not trying to take over or to ignore your authority. I'm just doing what I do, fixing messes before they do damage."

He waited for her to soften.

She squared her shoulders and crossed her arms over her chest.

"I'm sorry. I really am," he offered, trying a different tack. "It sucked seeing your showroom vandalized. You've got a nice, warm place here. Classy and upscale. You've obviously put a lot of time and energy into creating it. I hated seeing how hurt you were when someone screwed it up like that."

Her eyes softened for a second, the blue warming. Max relaxed, wondering if he should push his luck and reach out, brush his fingers over the smooth curve of her cheek. Rub a lock of her silky black hair, trail his palm over her shoulder. God, he really, really needed to touch her.

But first, he'd ask her out. On a real date, not some bullshit obligatory drink.

She wet her mouth, her teeth vividly white against the dusky rose of her lip color. She didn't drop her arms, but he saw some of the stiffness leave her shoulders.

Home free, he thought. He wondered if she'd like to have drinks before dinner, or after.

She leaned closer, her eyes locked on his. Max's pulse jumped, his heart rate spiking.

"I appreciate that you wanted to help," she said. Her words were soft, so soft that he barely caught the underlying fury in her tone. "But I can handle my business myself. I don't need you, or my brother, fixing things for me."

"It's not like I did an end run around you and hired someone. I saw you had a problem. Trying to be a nice guy, I asked around, got a few references and called in a couple favors to get you appointments ASAP."

"I appreciate that you're trying to be a nice guy."

There, maybe she was through with her tantrum and ready to show a little reasonable gratitude.

His smile had barely formed when she stepped forward, closing those last inches between them and poking her finger into his chest.

"But I'd be grateful if instead you'd work on being a nice guy who doesn't try to take over things that are none of his business."

That finger was the last straw. He wrapped his hand around it. She trembled. It was that tiny suggestion of vulnerability that made him look deeper. Past the stubborn set of her shoulders, the pride in her eyes. To the hints of hesitant fear. The way her teeth nibbled on her bottom lip. The slight frown between her brows. And there, in the blue depths of her eyes, the insecurity.

Max didn't understand how a woman this glorious could have an ounce of insecurity. He did know that the sight of it made him crazy.

Unable to resist, he lifted her hand to his lips. His eyes holding hers captive, he nibbled little kisses over the delicate bones of her knuckles.

Her skin was like silk. Her eyes narrowed. He breathed in her scent, letting it wash over him like a caress. His blood heated.

He turned her hand over in his, pressing his mouth to her open palm. Her lips trembled as she sucked in a breath. He scraped his teeth along the soft inside flesh of the finger she'd poked into his chest.

She made the softest, sexiest mewling sound in the back of her throat. His body hardened.

Still holding her eyes, he traced his tongue from the tip of her French manicure, down the slender length of her finger to the crux where her fingers met. Smiling a little, he flicked his tongue there, in the juncture.

Her eyes blurred. She gave a delicate shudder. His dick

pressed painfully against the zipper of his jeans, throbbing in a plea to be set free.

He sucked her finger into his mouth. He slid his tongue along the top, then the sides. Her tiny little moan was all he needed to hear.

Through playing, he lowered her hand from his mouth and pressed it against his racing heart. Before he could shove his own fingers into that thick fall of hair, though, there was a cough in the doorway.

They both froze. Sophia winced then tried to pull her hand away but he held tight.

He wasn't finished, dammit.

"Soph?" Gina broke in uncertainly. "There's a dude in a suit here for you. Said he's a P.I. here about a security consultation."

"Son of a—"

"A suit?" Sophia said dazedly, interrupting Max's oath. She frowned, then puffed out a breath and gave him an arch look. "Interesting timing."

"Isn't it just," he agreed with a rueful laugh. He waited for her to tell the Goth pixie to send the guy away.

Sophia's gaze shifted to his mouth for just a second, then she pressed her lips together and took a deep breath. He almost cried when the move made the silky black fabric of her blouse accentuate her lush curves.

"Tell him I'll be right there," Sophia instructed.

"What?" he yelped.

She slowly pulled her hand away, as if the wrong move could cause an explosion. Her eyes met his. He saw confusion and fear beneath the still flaming passion in her pale gaze.

Before he could assure her that they'd pick up after she was finished with the security contractor, she blinked. When those lush lashes lifted again, her eyes were veiled. Chilly.

He hated how she did that.

"Reschedule," he said softly, unable to stop the words even

though he knew it was one short step beneath begging. If she walked out, there was a damned good chance he'd have to work twice as hard to get back to this point.

"No." She nodded for Gina to go, then gave Max an indecipherable look. "You're the one who insisted I see him, after all. You might consider this a reward for your good deed."

Passion still raging through his system, Max rocked back on his heels and watched her sweep out of the room. He waited until she got to the door and murmured, "But I haven't done the deed with you, yet, sweetheart."

The hitch in her step was barely noticeable. But he grinned when he saw it.

THREE HOURS AFTER HER confrontation with Max, Sophia could still remember the feel of his mouth on her finger. Hot. Wet. Intense. She'd almost melted at his feet. Hell, she was ready to melt at just remembering how it'd felt. Who needed a pulsing shower massage when just the thought of Max's mouth on her finger got her juices flowing?

She'd barely heard the first investigator's questions, with all that passion still swimming through her head. She'd wanted to shove him out the door, flip the locks and rush back to her office to finish what Max had started.

By the second guy's pitch, she'd gone from meltingly horny to irritatedly frustrated. She'd been so busy inventing creative ways to emasculate Max, she hadn't listened to a word this P.I. had said, either.

By the third she'd found Zen. That peaceful place of acceptance, where she could release the anger and lust. It had been a mistake, but it was only a problem if she let it be. As long as she let all thoughts of Max and sex go, she'd be fine. So she'd spent that investigator's pitch time focusing on meditative breathing and images of ice water.

Pretty much all she remembered from the three meetings was that the men all thought her problems were personal, that they probably tied into her upcoming show and that it'd cost her a lot of money she didn't have for them to stake out her gallery, poke through her files and interview potential suspects.

Reaching her office, Sophia wanted nothing more than to kick off her shoes and relax. Before she'd stepped past the threshold, she knew those were impossible dreams.

Well, there went her freaking Zen.

"What're you still doing here?" she blurted out.

"Waiting for you." Max shifted on her couch, angling one arm along the long tapestry back and patting it in invitation. His smile was all charming welcome.

She wanted to throw something again.

And she was deathly afraid that something was herself, right into his arms.

"This entire time?" No man had ever waited for her.

"Most of it. I did run across the street and order some lunch," he said, pointing at the takeout cartons on the little table by the sofa. "I made some phone calls. I took a nap."

"A nap?" Her eyes drifted to the tasseled pillow leaning against the arm of the sofa, its blue silk invitingly indented. The same pillow she often laid her head on while daydreaming. Schoolgirl giddiness made her want to grab it up and hold it to her chest while she giggled.

He'd slept on her pillow.

Crazy. This situation was crazy, and so was she for not telling him to get off her couch, to leave her office and get the hell out of her life.

He was bossy and domineering. He didn't know how to take no for an answer. He was a man for whom the term chain of command was ingrained, with himself at the top of the chain.

He was the sexiest, most incredible man she'd ever met. He brought her to the edge of an orgasm by nibbling on her finger. Her finger, for crying out loud. And she wanted him like she'd never, ever wanted anyone, *anything,* in her life.

"So?" he asked expectantly, leaning back on the sofa and propping the ankle of one leg on the knee of the other.

Could he read her thoughts? Were they that obvious?

"So...?"

"So are you going to eat with me?" he clarified with a charming smile. "Gina said you were wrapping up, so I picked the food up about five minutes ago. It's still hot."

Sophia stood in the doorway, her eyes huge as she nibbled at her bottom lip.

He had no idea how difficult this choice was for her.

If she agreed, it would be to more than just lunch and they both knew it. How much more wasn't clear. But for her, if she opened the door, she wouldn't be able to resist going through it. Max had so many strikes against him. He was rich and bossy, like her late husband. He was handpicked by her brother, and she tried not to encourage her family's interference. He was sexy as hell, gorgeous and charm personified. And he was a danger to her heart. Where she'd thought Joseph was her Prince Charming, Max was easily a warrior knight.

It was like choosing between the temptation of the frying pan or the fire.

And maybe, just maybe, that's all she needed. After all, if she was the only one who realized they were about to have an incendiary, wildly passionate affair, that put her on top. That, and she could use his guaranteed expiration date—he'd be leaving in a month—to keep herself from doing anything too crazy. Like fall for the guy.

She let her gaze roam Max's gorgeous body as he sat, patiently waiting for her answer. From his tidy, military short hair and his laughing brown eyes to the rock-hard breadth of his shoulders. His long, long legs wrapped so lovingly in worn denim. And—call her silly for buying into all the myths, but oh, yeah, baby—his promisingly large feet.

She had a feeling being on top of Max was going to be one helluva ride.

6

SOPHIA PRESSED HER HAND to her stomach, trying to keep the wildly dancing nerves at bay. She couldn't believe she was actually going on a date. Oh, my God, a date.

She was crazy. She was in no position to date right now. She should be focusing on the gallery and the upcoming show, not wondering if she'd get laid.

Despite that, she hadn't been able to say no when Max had invited her to dinner.

"Yowza, hot stuff."

Halfway down the rickety staircase that led from her tiny apartment to the storage room of the gallery, Sophia grinned at Gina.

"You like?"

She reached the bottom step. Then, a little giddy over the evening ahead, she gave a sweeping turn to show off her dress.

It was black. It was shimmery. It was tiny.

It was perfect. From the barely there rhinestone straps to the subtle sheen of the fabric criss-crossing her breasts, to the cut-to-there handkerchief hem that offered teasing glimpses of her thighs when she moved.

It was a dress that said confident sex.

Sophia wanted to giggle. It felt so good to dress up and feel this good.

Her wardrobe over the past half year had consisted of business casual, exercise gear and jeans. None of which screamed sexy date. With no room in her tiny apartment for most of her belongings, she'd left the bulk of her wardrobe at the estate until Joseph's will was settled. Lynn's lawyers had insisted that Sophia vacate the house while the will was in probate. So she'd cleared it with Olivia and gone to the estate to raid her old closet.

"You look fab," Gina exclaimed. "I've seen you dressed up plenty of times for shows, but never so…"

"Sexy?"

Please.

Sophia held her breath.

"Oh, yeah, definitely sexy. Soldier boy isn't going to know what hit him."

"Perfect." The more shell-shocked Max was, the easier it would be for Sophia to hold the upper hand. Since her agreement the previous day to have dinner with him, all she'd been able to think about was him. His smile. His tight butt. His broad shoulders. His laugh. And most of all, his bossy nature.

Her buzzword of the night: control.

"Are you going to sleep with him?"

"Gina!" she gasped.

Her assistant just arched a brow, then dug into the bib pocket of her overalls. With a smirk, she held out a condom.

"Just in case."

Sophia's mouth worked but no words came out. She didn't even know if she was going to sleep with Max. Yes, she wanted to, but that didn't mean she would. Heat warmed her cheeks, caused, no doubt by her suddenly overworked heart. She couldn't take a condom. It was like holding up a sign that said

Horny Woman, Let's Rock. She'd never been that blatant. She'd always been more the please-sweep-me-off-my-feet type.

"C'mon, Soph."

"But… I don't know if I'm going to sleep with him," she admitted, nibbling the gloss off her lower lip.

"It's not like carrying a condom says, 'Let's screw,'" Gina patiently instructed. "No more than having auto insurance says you're going to drive like an idiot. It's, you know, just in case."

Sophia shook her head. No. This was their first date, so no matter how smart insurance might be, nobody was driving tonight. Before she could say anything, though, there was a knock on the side door.

"That's Max," she said, pressing a hand to her stomach. Then she tasted the sweetness of her lipstick on her teeth, worn off from nibbling on her lip. "I have to fix my face. Can you let him in?"

"Sure." Gina offered an encouraging smile and turned to leave.

"Wait!"

She was the one who wanted to take control of her life. Which meant carrying insurance, dammit. Sophia hurried to catch up with the other woman. Not slowing her pace or looking back, Gina held the condom over her shoulder.

Just because she had no plans to drive didn't mean she might not kick a few tires.

And this way, she was making the decision. Any sweeping would be done by her, thank you very much.

Five minutes later, she joined Max and Gina in the showroom. She almost tripped in her Jimmy Choos at the sight of him.

Madre de Dios, the man was gorgeous. As he was half turned away from her, she took a moment to appreciate how well his black slacks cupped his butt, just visible beneath the sport jacket. At her sigh of appreciation, he turned and offered a welcoming smile. His dress shirt was open at the collar, the deep red almost as dark as his slacks. Her heart stuttered a few times as she tried to regain her composure.

"Hello, Max," she said. "You look wonderful."

"I think that's my line," he said with a laugh, stepping forward to take her hand. She wet her lips, glad that her fingers didn't tremble in his, despite the delicious warmth swirling up her arm. Then he lifted her hand to his lips, pressing a soft kiss against her knuckles. Her insides melted into a gooey puddle of lust. "Sophia, you take my breath away."

She stared into his eyes, the chocolate depths assuring her that he was, indeed, as hooked as she was.

Oh, yeah, she realized, watching that lecture in her brain explode in a puff of smoke. This was definitely about right now. And right now was going to feel damned good.

A half hour later, she and Max were surrounded by more romantic lighting, this time from candlelit tables. Sophia followed their host, painfully aware of Max just a couple of steps behind. Watching her butt, she'd noticed.

Should she walk a little stiffer so he didn't think she was enticing him?

Or should she put a little swing in her hips, and hope that made him a little stiffer?

She noticed women left and right were eyeing him, casting warm looks, and one even tried a little finger wiggle. As if Sophia was blind? Risking a quick glance over her shoulder, Sophia noted the appreciation on his face. Not for the women, whom he clearly didn't notice. Nope, his eyes were firmly fixed on her butt.

Yeah. Swing it was.

"What a lovely restaurant," she said, offering her thanks to the waiter as he seated her. "I've seen reviews in the *Chronicle,* but haven't eaten here before. From what I've heard, though, getting a last-minute reservation is harder than getting elected governor."

Max grinned, taking the wine list from the host, then immediately ordering without looking at it. As soon as the host thanked him and left, Max reached across the burgundy tablecloth to take her hand.

"One of my cousins works here," he admitted, playing with her fingers. "I used the family card."

"Nice," she said, laughing a little breathlessly. His touch reminded her of how he'd made her feel the previous day. Pretending her body wasn't melting in his presence, she glanced around. Eying the staff, she wondered which one was his cousin. Guy or gal? "Isn't it nice when family actually comes in handy?"

"Nice, and rare." She glanced back just in time to see an exhausted sort of resignation flash in his eyes. Since she often felt the same when it came to her relatives, she turned her hand to curl her fingers companionably into his. For the first time since he'd walked in on her and the giant penis, she saw him as more than a sexy pain in her ass.

Was his family as much a stressfest for him as hers was for her? Sophia had spent most of her life on a teeter-totter of love versus resentment with her family. Maybe they had something other than lust in common.

She looked at him, all sexy and strong, with that charming grin and glint in his dark eyes. She sighed, glad she'd been brave enough to come tonight.

"What a great table," she murmured, glancing at the view of the city from the wide plateglass window.

"It's all about connections," he said with a shrug.

"Like your connections were handy yesterday afternoon?" she asked, referring to the private investigators who'd paraded through her gallery.

His grin widened. He tried to hide it by lifting her hand to his lips and pressing a kiss on her knuckles, but Sophia caught it despite the lusty surge swirling through her tummy.

"I thought my connections yesterday were put to pretty

good use," he pointed out, arching one brow as he nibbled at her fingertips.

"I think you wasted those men's time, since I can't hire any of them," she told him.

"I wasn't talking about the investigators."

"You're incorrigible," she said, laughing despite herself. Not sure how to handle this weird combination of desire and amusement, she pulled her fingers from his to play with her fork.

She'd agreed to this date in a fog of lust and she was pretty sure, since he'd insisted they have it this evening, that Max knew that. Despite her sexy fantasies, she hadn't been sure the evening would be much more than stilted small talk, a good dinner and maybe another one of those sexy kisses when he walked her to her door.

But now? Now she was pretty sure her lusty hit-and-run was starting to turn into something more. Something a little deeper, a little scarier. Infatuation, she told herself. Nothing to back away from. She could like the guy, admire him for more than his tight butt and gorgeous eyes and still want to jump his bones, right?

Sophia's breath shuddered a little as she contemplated just how great that jumping was going to feel. From the admiring look in his eyes, the jumping was going to feel incredible for both of them.

"YOU LOOK LIKE YOU'RE contemplating the fate of nations," Max teased, wondering what had put that intense look on Sophia's face.

Her eyes met his. The heated curiosity in those blue depths damn near melted his shorts. It was a look that said maybe. His body responded to maybe with definite hardening. His shoulders straightened. His abs flattened. His dick lengthened.

Slow down, he reminded himself. First-date rules meant his dick wouldn't be getting any play tonight.

He wondered how soon they could have a second date.

"It's not the fate of nations I'm considering," she finally responded with a smile that put his resolve to the test. "Much littler fates, actually."

Well, his fate wasn't little, that was for damned sure. Resisting the urge to tell—or offer to show—her, he smiled instead and cast his brain around for some way to cool things down.

"So your family," he said, grasping for a safe topic. "They aren't involved with your gallery?"

Well, it wasn't an ice bath, but there was definitely a little chill at the table now. Her eyes no longer promising the key to sexual nirvana, Sophia leaned back a ways.

"My family isn't crazy about the gallery," she admitted in a tone that was too casual to hide the hurt underneath.

"They don't approve?"

She hesitated, then shrugged. "Let's just say they felt keeping a distance would keep the peace."

"Because you like to run your business your own way?"

"Oh, wouldn't that be sweet," she said, her words low and reverential, as if she were offering up a prayer.

What did she mean by that? And why did she look so sad?

Before he could ask, their waiter arrived with a basket of bread, a tray of dipping oils and his order pad.

Max leaned forward to resume his interrogation… No, the discussion.

"I love this bread. You can always tell a good restaurant by the quality of their bread, don't you think?" she said before he could voice his question. "Had you discovered it before or was it through your cousin that you found it?"

Bread? Was that the best she could do? Max narrowed his eyes, noting her arched brow and closed look. Change of subject it was, then.

"One of the guys in the paratrooper squad grew up in the

area. On his recommendation, I tried it last year when I was home on leave. My cousin getting a job here was just coincidence. One that worked pretty well," Max admitted, "since it got us reservations."

Her smile warmed him. A reward for following topic directions? She dipped a small piece of bread into the basil oil and made a seductive little humming noise when she tasted it. Max almost groaned. The woman was pure sensuality. He couldn't wait to hear the sound she made when he kissed her. Would she moan? Sigh? Give one of those sexy little growls?

To distract himself, he broke off a piece of bread and asked, "So what'd you think of the investigators? Which one will you hire?"

"I told you already, none of them. I appreciate your trying to help, but I'll take care of the gallery myself. Like you said, the police are investigating."

Irritation simmered in his gut. Was she so stubborn she wouldn't hire a professional? What the hell kind of business-woman did that? Rico had been right when he'd said she needed looking after.

Then he looked past the proud tilt of her chin and saw the worry in her eyes. Maybe she couldn't afford a P.I., which made him a jerk to keep pushing the subject. He wanted to help her, not make her feel bad.

Thankfully the waiter chose that moment to deliver their meals. Max waited until the plates had been settled and she'd had her first bite.

"If there's anything I can do to help…"

"Thanks. But why don't we talk about something besides my business issues," she suggested with a tight smile.

Max considered. He didn't mind pushing if he thought it'd get him what he wanted. But his goal wasn't to piss Sophia off, or to simply get answers. It was to find out who was behind her vandalism problems. He could do that and stay on her good side.

Starting first thing in the morning, he'd simply become her stand-in P.I. He'd hang out, keep an eye on things. He'd ask questions and figure out who was causing problems. And Sophia wouldn't have a clue. Which meant she wouldn't get pissed.

Although the flying sparks might have been fun. He definitely liked the way she stated her mind. It was damned sexy to have someone strong enough to tell him how she liked it. He wondered if she carried that habit into the bedroom.

And how long it'd take him to find out.

"Sure," Max said agreeably. "So who's von Schilling?"

Sophia fumbled her fork. He winced, glad that the spaghetti didn't slide off the tines and land in her lap.

"What do you know about von Schilling?" she accused, her eyes shimmering with suspicion.

"It depends," he said, slicing one of the huge meatballs into quarters and forking up a bite. "If it's Hans von Schilling the photographer, which would make sense given your gallery, then I know a bit. He rose to fame in the sixties with his show chronicling the seedy side of flower power. He ostensibly retired fifteen years ago, becoming a recluse in the past decade."

The candlelight glistened off her lower lip in a very appealing way as her mouth hung open.

"My parents were contemporaries of his," Max explained. Most boys got their first eyeful of naked women sneaking a peek at their dad's *Playboy* stash. At nine, Max had gotten his at one of von Schilling's shows. The man had a way with the naked lady pictures, Max remembered fondly. "My father more than my mother, I think."

She set her fork down. Probably a good idea since her pasta was looking pretty precarious.

"Nice summary," she acknowledged. "But I meant why would you ask me, specifically, about von Schilling?"

"Because his rep called while I was waiting in your office."

Blue eyes huge with shock, her mouth worked. It took her a few tries to find the words, though. "You answered my phone?"

Forking up another meatball, Max shook his head. "Of course not. I listened to the message he left on your machine."

She tapped those sexy fingers on the table, the move shaking her knife against its neighboring spoon in a gentle medley of irritation. Her eyes narrowed in irritation. Why? He hadn't poked through her drawers. He hadn't answered the phone, even though he had a personal history with the caller. And hadn't he just backed down instead of pushing her to hire someone to patrol her building?

None of that came easy for him. But he was a soldier who knew how to assess a situation. And a man wasn't raised by Tabby St. James without learning a thing or two about biding his time and picking his battles when it came to women. So he ate his spaghetti and waited.

He hadn't eaten more than a mouthful before Sophia had enough of the finger-tapping. She pressed those sexy fingers flat on the cloth and leaned toward him.

He prepared himself for the tirade.

"How would you summarize von Schilling's work?" she asked in the same tone one of his squad mates would use asking how he'd assess a ticking bomb.

Even though he had no clue what was going on, Max set his fork down to give her question the attention it deserved.

"Von Schilling. Brilliant composition, a mastery of mood, quirky humor beneath the edgy realism."

She nodded. The huge smile that curved her mouth was so beautiful, he felt as if he'd been hit upside the head. Max had to lean back in his chair to catch his breath. Damn, she was gorgeous.

"He's my hero," she said enthusiastically. "I've studied his work. He sees the soul through the lens of his camera. His photo essay of the European cities was so evocative, it drove me to study in Paris for a year. That's how I started specializing in candid pictures of faces. Not portraits. Portraits are usually masks. Candids give peeks into the soul."

Her eyes shone with a passion that made him wish he could see her visions. She was amazing. There was passion, yes. And that was a total turn-on. But it was the compassion there that really got to him.

"Why aren't you showing your photos?" he asked. He wasn't an art buff, and he'd only seen a couple of snapshots from her camera view window, but they'd looked good to him.

The question shut her down, though. As if watching someone pull the shades on a sunny day, he could see her enthusiasm dim.

"No. My work isn't show-worthy," she dismissed. "Nothing even close to von Schilling's caliber."

"I'll introduce you," Max offered without a clue how he'd pull it off. The guy lived in a fortress in Santa Cruz, and for all Max knew, he hadn't welcomed visitors in years. Would he even remember an old acquaintance's gawking kid? Didn't matter. Max loved the way her eyes had lit up, and he was going to make it happen for her.

"Thanks, but I don't need an introduction," Sophia replied, chopping his white knight impulse off at the knees. "His rep has called the gallery a few times over the past month. From the sound of it, he's willing to meet anytime."

"You don't sound enthusiastic."

"I'm not. I turned down the meeting." As if talking about it ruined her appetite, she wrinkled her nose and set her fork and knife across the plate.

"Why?" Since his plate was all but licked clean, Max laid down his utensils, too, folded his arms along the edge of the table and leaned forward. "You said he's your hero. From the sound of that message, he obviously wants to work with you. What's the problem?"

Her sigh did lovely things to the glittery fabric of her dress. Max's own sigh was pure appreciation as he watched the candlelight.

"While he's delved into a variety of subjects, he specializes in nudes. Women."

Oh, yeah, he nodded fondly. He'd been totally thrilled to discover just that fact. "I remember."

Sophia gave a little roll of her eyes, shaking her head in typical female pity. But she smiled anyway.

"Since taking over the gallery, I've put all my energies into returning the gallery to its pre-erotic days. A show featuring naked woman in compromising positions would be a step in the wrong direction."

Max shifted to attention. "How long had the gallery focused on erotica?"

"Four years."

"Was that a lucrative focus?"

"Haven't you heard? Scx sells." She leaned closer. Her dress was fitted closely, so it didn't gape, more the pity. It did, however, allow the candle to cast a tempting shadow, one he wanted to trace along the silky curve of her breasts. She gave a vampy flutter of her lashes. "Four-foot marble penises, fornicating copper couples, blown glass cli…" She trailed off with a little wince, then shrugged. "Let's just say there's definitely a market."

He grinned. A woman who'd spent four or so years in a gallery that sold naughty bits blushed when discussing them. She was so sweet.

"And you recently shifted focus?" he clarified. "You let all those artists go?"

"I recently returned focus to the gallery's original, historic objective. To feature the best of California photographs and photographers," she explained. "And we don't hire the artists. We show their work on commission. And yes, I've released all of the pieces as their contracts expired."

Just as he'd thought. She was just too close to see the obvious. You'd think the cops would've caught on, though.

"Did you ever think that's where your vandalism might be coming from?" He shifted, resting his arm along the back of his chair, waiting for her praise and gratitude.

Her hair slid like a heavy black silk curtain, covering one sexy shoulder as she tilted her head to the side. Her smile was a little stiffer now. Embarrassed that he'd figured it out so easily? Reassuring her would probably only add to her discomfort, so he waited.

"Actually, I did think of that," she said. Max frowned. Were they on the same page, then? "Gina and I checked into the artists, and all seem to be doing really well. Nobody was hurt by the decision, nobody has any reason to resent the change."

"You're kidding? Nobody's pissed? No one's holding a grudge?"

A shadow flickered in her eyes for a brief second, then she blinked and it was gone.

"I'm sure whoever is behind the vandalism isn't an artist," she assured him.

Max frowned. He thought she was wrong. But he knew he couldn't convince her without getting her pissed off. And pissing Sophia off would definitely ruin his plans for the rest of the evening.

Max struggled with his need to push, to grab hold of her business situation and fix it for her. He could clearly see the challenge in her eyes. If he pushed, she'd push right back. And not in a sexy, pleasurable way.

His two most vital urges battled. The need to fix a problem versus the need to romance a beautiful woman.

"Dessert?"

Max gave the waiter a grateful smile. Good timing. He had no doubt he'd be able to fix Sophia's business issues. But tonight wasn't about that. Tonight was about the two of them.

The two of them, and dessert.

That's what mattered.

He'd fix all her problems tomorrow.

7

"THANKS FOR THE WONDERFUL evening," Sophia told Max as calmly as she could when he opened the passenger door and held out his hand to help her from the sleek black sports car. She was glad for the help, since her knees felt like jelly.

How did women stand this sexual tension stuff? It was making her a nervous wreck.

"I'm glad you enjoyed dinner," he said as he walked her the half-dozen steps from where he'd parked to the polished oak railing of the staircase leading up to her apartment.

They both glanced up at the well-lit landing, the lush dieffenbachia in a wicker basket glinting softly in the lamplight.

"I'd like to see you again," he said, his hand on her arm preventing her from heading up the stairs.

Was this it? Their date was over? But…she had condoms. They couldn't be done yet.

Sophia stared up into his eyes, the amused charm matching his tone of voice. She flushed, her breath catching in her throat at the look in those dark depths.

Definitely desire. Appreciation, respect, amusement. Nice as those were, it was the desire she focused on.

He made her want. Want pleasure, want satisfaction, want

him. Want it all. She could hear Gina's voice, urging her to grab on for the ride. But for all her yearnings to feel those things with Max, she wasn't sure how to handle this. How to ask him.

A part of her wanted to cry because he'd slowed things down enough that her brain could overrule her hormones. Another part of her, the part that had ruled her life for twenty-five years, was grateful. She needed to be careful. To be cautious. To not humiliate herself.

And given her lack of sexual experience, there was a distinct possibility that humiliation could go hand in hand with the naked tangling she'd been imagining.

Just as well to skip it.

"Actually," she said quietly, "I'm going to be really busy for the next week or so. The gallery has a show this weekend and that and the ensuing sales and work will take up most of my time."

"I'd imagine a show takes a great deal of time and energy." He shifted his gaze from her to glance toward the front of the gallery and he nodded agreeably. "But maybe you'll have a spare hour here or there for drinks or lunch?"

The temptation was overwhelming. The same as when her father had promised her a week in Santa Cruz, sans overprotective brothers, if she graduated magna cum laude. Or when Joseph had offered to let her run the gallery as soon as she received her master's in fine art. But neither man had followed through on their promise. Oh, her father had tried, but Diego had followed her to Santa Cruz anyway. And Joseph? He'd never kept promises.

So she'd be crazy to give in to the temptation to see their relationship as...well, a potential relationship and not just an option for hot and wild sex. Wouldn't she?

He was asking her to continue seeing him. To date. To build a relationship. With a man who, yes, turned her on like crazy, but also challenged what mattered most. Her control. Over herself, over her life.

One night, she might be able to handle.

More than an evening of decadent pleasure? She'd have to be crazy. He was overwhelming, and much too much like the other men in her life for her sanity.

Besides, what if she sucked at the pleasure stuff? All she had to go on was her sex life with Joseph. And if that was any measure, she was severely lacking.

Apparently one of Max's myriad skills was the ability to read faces. Noting the regret on hers, he smiled and shrugged.

"Think about it, okay?" He gave one of those guy head nods that spoke volumes. Acceptance, regret and still that lingering desire. Sophia wanted to throw her purse on the ground, kick her feet and have a tantrum. Dammit, couldn't she have the desire without all the baggage?

"I guess this is good night, then," he said, stepping closer, his hand briefly taking hers before moving up her arm to rest on her shoulder. Hearing the regret in his voice, Sophia felt something inside her shift.

"No," she told him, wetting her lips nervously. Terrified excitement buzzed in her ears. A little light-headed, as if she'd just guzzled a magnum of champagne, she reached out to rub the lapel of his jacket between her fingers.

His smile had a hint of wickedness, at war with the sudden caution in his eyes.

"You don't want me to leave?"

"I want you to come up," she said, as close to innuendo as she could get.

"For a drink?" he clarified, stepping closer. Without thinking, Sophia stepped back, her spine plastering itself to the brick wall of her building.

Sophia swallowed hard, then forced herself to meet his eyes. "For the night."

She knew her words had an effect. She was close enough to feel him suck in a surprised breath as his fingers briefly clenched her shoulders. But his charming smile and that mellow look in his eyes didn't change.

Sophia lifted her chin, promising herself that once she got him upstairs, she'd damn well break that control of his. Even if she had to dance on his face to do it.

"You're asking me upstairs...for the night?"

"Yes." Sensing a little gentlemanly reluctance, she bit her lip and took a chance. Reaching out, she tiptoed her fingers up his chest. Then, her eyes locked on his, she slid her fingernails back down in a teasingly erotic caress.

His eyes narrowed.

"And you're asking me upstairs, specifically, for sex," he said slowly, his blunt terms no doubt meant to shock her into... What? Thinking twice?

Instead, the raw words sent a shaft of heat through her. Sophia pressed her thighs tight against each other, the satiny slide of her hose adding an extra punch of delicious pleasure.

"I'm suggesting we go upstairs and keep our minds open to the myriad of possible...positions—" she paused, running her tongue over her bottom lip "—we might find ourselves in."

His heart pounded against her fingertips.

"And, believe me, it pains me to even ask this, but after we see what comes up, shall we say, you expect me to just walk away?"

Her lips twitched at his innuendo. She tilted her head in question, the sensual caress of her own hair sliding over her oversensitized skin adding another layer of pleasure.

"I'm saying that we have an opportunity to enjoy ourselves. And if you're interested in a short visit, then I'd love to chat." She bit her lip. A part of her wanted to promise to spend his entire leave rolling around together naked. But even though she wanted him like crazy, the two main issues remained.

One, he was undoubtedly bad for her. And two, what if she sucked in bed? She'd rather not see him after sunup if that proved to be the case. Better safe than sorry.

"As for tomorrow," she finally said, "we're both busy. You have family commitments. I have a show coming up that needs all my attention. Why put the pressure of promises on either of us?"

His groan was almost silent, but she felt it anyway and grinned.

"I don't know if I can—"

A quick thrill of panic pushed Sophia right out of her comfort zone and into bold sauciness. She let her hand trail down his rock-hard abs, almost groaning herself at the feel of them, over the leather strip of his belt. Then she cupped her palm over his zipper and grinned at the large bulge pressing against her hand.

"Oh, I definitely think you can."

His laugh was a little breathless, a smidge desperate. It was all Sophia needed to hear. She felt more powerful than she'd ever imagined she could. She could climb mountains. Slay dragons. Blow Sergeant Maximilian St. James right here in the alley leading up to her apartment.

Or better, tempt him up those stairs where he'd show her delights she'd spent years wondering about. Did he do all those sexy things she'd read about? Nibble and lick and touch in the ways she'd dreamed of? Did he go down and did he like it? Would he let her try and would she like it?

It was as if a whole new world was right here, throbbing beneath her fingers. She leaned forward, trapping her hand between his heated length and her own body. On tiptoe, her free hand using his shoulder for balance, she pressed her mouth to his.

His lips parted, soft and welcoming. She licked the fullness, reveling in his taste. Wine, a hint of chocolate and something deeper, darker and ultimately more tempting that was all Max.

She couldn't let him refuse.

Tossing pride aside, for once not waiting for the guy to make the proper move, she took charge. After a quick, gentle nip at his lower lip, she slipped her tongue along his. Swirling and sliding.

He groaned, both hands sliding down her back to cup her butt. Fingers curved into her cheeks, he pulled her closer, lifted her higher.

Their tongues danced, slow at first. She gently sucked his into her mouth. He gave a low groan, his hands convulsing. He slid one in a gentle sweep up her back, curving his fingers behind her neck, cradling her head gently.

And then he got serious. The kiss went from tentative to intense with the stab of his tongue. They dueled. They danced. They delighted each other into going deeper, into wanting more.

It was a dance in which they both led. She tempted, he teased. She moaned, he laughed. His mouth, his hands, his body. She wanted them all.

Sophia had never felt like this. So sexy, so powerful. God, so ready to come.

Wet and throbbing, she rubbed against his throbbing erection, needing something, anything, to relieve the building pressure. His hand shifted, releasing her butt to gather the filmy fabric of her skirt. His fingers warmed her bare skin above the lacy elastic of her stockings.

Sophia moaned her approval, pressing her hand against his chest for support. She shifted, giving thanks to Pilates as she balanced on one leg, wrapping the other around his hard thigh.

"Upstairs," she breathed against his mouth.

He pulled back to stare at her, then closed his eyes as if he were trying to get a grip on his control. Nope, not what she wanted. Desperate to stay in control, and to get her way, she took his hand in hers, pressing it against her aching breast.

His groan was pure surrender.

She slowly slid her leg down his, making sure her heel grazed all the way down his thigh and calf. He gave a little laugh, the helpless kind that sent a shaft of excitement through her ego. He met her eyes with a dark, intense look that promised her the night of her life.

"You're determined to drive me crazy, aren't you?"

"Yes," she confirmed with a wicked smile.

Still holding his hand, she turned and pulled him up the stairs with her. She could feel the warmth of his gaze on her swinging hips as if it was a physical thing. Her knees trembled. Excitement, she told herself. There was nothing to worry about.

She was calling the shots tonight.

She was barely aware of taking her keys out and opening the door. So ingrained were her manners, she was sure she said something to welcome him to her apartment, but for the life of her, she had no clue what it was.

As soon as he closed the door, she pounced. With the living room illuminated only by the porch light dimly shining through the lace curtains, she grabbed Max by his lapels and steered him toward the couch. Once there, all it took was a gentle push to send him lying flat, his grin glinting in the dark room.

Thankful for her floaty skirt, she straddled his body. Palms flat on his belly, she pressed them up the hard planes of his chest and gripped his solidly muscled shoulders.

"Yum," she murmured as she leaned down to brush a soft, open-mouthed kiss over his chin. "I'll bet you're even tastier than dessert."

"I don't know," he said, his hands sliding up her stockings and under the fluttery handkerchief hem of her dress. Sophia shivered at his touch, his fingers making her thighs tingle with desire. "That was a damned good dessert. You might want to do a lot of tasting to compare."

"I'm a dessert expert," she declared, nibbling down his throat and breathing deeply. God, he smelled good. Hot, spicy male. She breathed deep, noting no cologne. Just a hint of soap, shaving cream and Max himself. Delicious.

His shirt was in the way. With nimble fingers, she unbuttoned the crisp cotton. When she reached his belly—and oh, God, who knew bellies could be that toned?—she tugged the fabric from his slacks. He lifted his torso so she could shove his shirt and jacket off his shoulders. Those incredible abs contracted. Sophia whimpered. His body was a work of art. And she had a great appreciation for art.

She needed to touch. To taste. She waited until he'd tossed his shirt and jacket aside before pouncing.

Her thighs gripping his hips, she nibbled her way down his throat again, flicking her fingers over a nipple. He groaned. She flicked again. She ran her tongue over the other nipple, then scraped her nails gently over his belly.

The feeling was incredible. Free reign to enjoy his body, to let herself do, taste, have, anything she wanted. Power mixed with pleasure, both sending tighter swirls of desire deep between her legs.

His hands gripped her thighs, this time a little rougher. She gasped. What was he going to do? Where would he touch? Her heart pounded in anticipation. He curved his fingers over her butt, then continued the upward motion under her dress to her waist.

Getting the hint, Sophia straightened. She reached across her chest, her arm brushing the already aching tips of her breasts as she unhooked, then lowered the side zipper of her dress. She looked down at him, raising her arms in silent command.

Deliciously obedient, he slid his hands higher, pulling the

fabric over her head and tossing it somewhere in the direction of his shirt.

Sophia slowly lowered her arms. Swallowing her nerves, she pretended she wasn't self-conscious of his gaze on her almost-naked body.

"Oh, sweetheart," he breathed, his fingers skimming a heated trail over her shoulder, down her chest and over the lush curve of her breast to swirl a design around her aching nipple. He blazed the same trail down the other side of her chest, this time brushing the tips of his fingers over her hardening tip. Then with both hands, he cupped her heavy breasts in his palms as if paying homage to their weight. She squirmed, hot desire dampening her panties. The move taunted, tormented and brought a hint of relief to her aching body.

Time to kick this into high gear, she decided.

She shimmied down his body, keeping the delicious pressure of his hard thigh between her legs.

Sprinkling hot, wet kisses over his chest, she slid lower, still. Her teeth scraped over the beautiful definition of his abs. Her hands made quick work of his belt, then the snap of his pants.

The point of no return, she knew. And she also was positive she didn't want any returns. So she shoved his pants and boxers lower. She shifted, reluctantly ungripping his thigh with her own, to push the cloth down farther. With a quick move and talented toes, he kicked off his shoes, pants and socks.

Sophia grinned as he arched a brow.

"Impressive," she complimented.

"You ain't seen nothing yet," he promised.

Her eyes dropped to the huge, glistening length of his erection and she sighed. He was right. But she intended to see, touch, taste and experience it all before the night was over.

"Yum," she said again.

One of his hands curved over her back, the other brushed through her hair as she slid down his body again.

She blew on the tip of his dick, smiling at the mercurial response as it gave a little jump. She swirled her tongue over the head. He groaned. She sucked the velvety tip deep into her mouth.

"Uh-uh," he groaned before she could do much more. "We'll be through before we start if you keep that up."

"Keeping it up is your job, isn't it?" she asked with a naughty look.

He laughed, but still pulled her head away from his.

In a masterful move right out of a movie, he gripped her body and flipped their positions so she lay on the couch, the nubby fabric of the couch rough against her bare back. He loomed over her, his hot gaze scanning her body. Then he gave an appreciative hum of pleasure.

"You're gorgeous."

She'd never been called gorgeous before. It was a heady experience.

"Turnabout tasting time," he said in a husky tone, his intention clear on his face.

Sophia giggled. It was wildly inappropriate and would probably piss him off. But she couldn't help it. But Max grinned, his light laugh as much a turn-on as the hand he snaked down her body as if he was making a test run to see which erogenous zone he wanted to taste first.

His fingers brushed her nipple. Sophia sucked in a breath. Apparently that was all he needed to make his decision. He lowered his head, sucking one aching tip into his mouth. The intense power of his mouth on her body sent her spinning on a wave of desire.

"Your bedroom," he muttered, his mouth sliding lower to her naked belly.

"This is it," she gasped.

He pulled his head back to frown at her, giving the large airy studio a quick glance. "Bed?"

"Couch pulls out," she said, shifting her hips to remind him that there were more important matters at hand.

He blinked as if trying to figure out a problem that just wouldn't compute. Then apparently realizing it didn't matter, he shrugged.

"At least we made it to the bed, then," he said before lowering his mouth again. His tongue snaked down to her belly button. His breath warmed the damp silk of her panties. She lifted her hips for him to pull them off. He just grinned and with a quick snap, ripped the fabric from her body.

Her eyes flew open in shock. Sophia swore she actually came a little. Her body constricted, wet and swollen. Her muscles tensed, even as her thighs fell apart to make room for his shoulders.

She shivered when he slid his hands beneath her hips, his fingers caressing her butt, lifting her higher. Anchoring her elbows for leverage, she lifted her head so it rested on the arm of the sofa. She had to watch him. Had to see, to stay in control.

His dark hair was so short, there was barely any tousled evidence that she'd ran her hands through it as he kissed his way down one thigh and then back up the other.

When he reached the crux of her legs, he glanced up and met her eyes. His were glinted with a hunger she'd never seen before. Desperate, wicked, intense. And all for her.

Holding her eyes, he leaned forward and licked the damp juices coating her swollen bud.

She shuddered, her fingers clenching the rounded strength of his shoulders. It was like grabbing rocks. The muscles were so hard, there was no give. Oh, baby, he had an incredible body.

As if he was making a wish, he blew out a puff of air, his

hot breath on her oversensitized flesh making her gasp. Then, apparently through teasing, he went to town.

He tasted her, his lips creating a delicious torment. Sophia dropped her head back, unable to think anymore with all the wild sensations he was showing her.

Intensifying her pleasure, he smoothed his other hand up her torso in a tingling caress. He cupped her breast, his fingers tweaking her nipple as his mouth drove her higher.

He slipped one finger into her. Then two. His fingers swirled, his tongue sipped.

Light exploding behind her eyes, she mewled her pleasure.

Sucking her swollen, aching bud into his mouth, he nipped gently as his fingers speared in, then out. In, then out.

She exploded in a burst of color and pleasure.

"Oh, God," she moaned over and over, her breath coming in pants that burned her throat. Pleasure pounded at her while lights burst behind her closed eyes. Stars. She swore she actually saw stars.

Max pressed a gentle kiss to the swollen bud he'd just tormented before laying his head on her belly and wrapping his arms around her hips in a hug that was both sexy and affectionate at the same time.

Her insides all melted together in a puddle of mind-blowing pleasure, she forced herself to move. This might be the only night she got with Max. She was going to make damned sure it was incredible.

For both of them.

Sliding her legs from under him, she shifted into a sitting position. His eyes heavy with desire, Max fell to the couch in the space she'd left, grabbing her hand to make sure she didn't go far. Lying there on his side, his head propped on his fist, he shook his head in protest.

"Come back," he murmured.

Her eyes traced the hard, delicious length of his body. From his sexy feet—when the hell had feet become sexy?—to the light dusting of hair on his muscled thighs. She swallowed hard when her eyes rested on his jutting erection. That marble statue had nothing on Max. Pure male perfection. She wanted to touch him, taste him again.

She forced her eyes to continue their journey up the drool-worthy planes of his six-pack to the hard span of his chest.

"You're perfect," she said, repeating the compliment back to him. And he was. His body was a work of art. A part of her wished for her camera to preserve this moment. To take it out later to savor. She wanted to know if his beauty was real, if this pleasure was as immense as her mind, and her body, were telling her.

She met his gaze and the need to analyze disappeared. For the first time in her life, she felt like she could trust her own eyes.

"Sophia?"

He sounded so sweet, so concerned. As if he'd picked up on every one of her fears and wanted to put them at ease. As if her emotional needs were just as important as her physical pleasure.

She handed over a tiny piece of her heart in that moment.

Insane. She knew better. She knew he couldn't be a part of her future.

But he was a part of her right now. And she had to believe that their lovemaking would only be that much better for a little love added to it.

Sophia gave him a reassuring smile and stood, crooking her finger to indicate he join her. His sigh was barely perceptible, but his smile didn't waver as he stood to join her.

"We're going to want a lot of room for this," she told him, quickly tossing the cushions aside so she could pull out the sofa bed. As soon as it was open, he grabbed her around the waist and pulled her down.

"Nice," he murmured. He pressed a kiss to her shoulder when they hit the mattress. She smiled and settled into the soft down ticking. She might have to sleep on a sofa bed, but she'd be damned if she'd be uncomfortable.

She'd stolen the feather topper off her bed at the estate.

And while soft was always a good thing, hard was even better. And she wanted Max's hard body beneath her.

With that in mind, she shifted, pressing her hands to his shoulders so he lay flat, his body tan against the pristine white of the sheets.

"Condom," he reminded her as she straddled him.

She reached over, the tip of her breast grazing his chest and sending another zing of pleasure through her as she grabbed her purse from the sofa table. Wasting no moves, she pulled one of the condoms Gina had given her from the tiny case, ripped it open and smoothed it over the hard, tempting length of his erection.

"Now," she told him.

Ranging herself up on her knees, she poised over his body. Needing to prove she could, she waited. One second, then two. Max curved his hands over her thighs, then with a little smile snapped the lace of the stockings she still wore.

She gave him what he wanted. What they both wanted. Slowly, as deliciously slow as she could, she lowered herself onto his straining erection. Hot and wet, she slid down in one swift, easy move.

"Mmm," she moaned. Riding him like the stud he was, she focused on the building pleasure. Each thrust was met with an undulating welcome. God, he felt good.

Pressure built. Passion intensified, an edgy cloud of excitement washing over her. Every fear she'd ever harbored about her sexuality vaporized as she felt the power of Max's desire for her.

Needing more, wanting it all, she took his hands and

pressed them to her aching breasts. His fingers teased, tormented, sending them both higher.

She thrust deeper, her inner walls gripping his dick as if she could milk every drop of pleasure from him.

Max groaned, his body convulsing beneath her. His fingers dug into the soft flesh of her ass. The intensity of his climax destroyed the last of Sophia's control. She threw back her head, her orgasm exploding through her. Panting, mewling and shuddering, she felt the pleasure in every atom of her being.

Spent and exhausted, she dropped. Her thighs slid flat against the mattress as her head hit his chest.

"You're right," he said eventually, his words a little breathless rumble against her ear.

"Right?" She didn't even know where she'd found the energy to speak. She was wrung empty.

"That was better than dessert."

She laughed, a soft giggle of delight, as she curled into his arms and drifted off to sleep, feeling smug and happy. She'd not only had the best sex of her life, she'd proved that she could have it, stay in control and still make the guy smile like he'd won the world's greatest orgasm sweepstakes.

It was only temporary, but it felt pretty damned good.

8

"WAIT A MINUTE," MAX said, his jacket in one hand, a cooling piece of toast in the other. "What's the deal?"

He'd been lucky to get his damn slacks zipped before Sophia had started making shooing motions to push him toward the front door.

"I have a crazy day and really need to get started," she was saying, looking a little crazy herself. Her hair had that wild, sex-all-night look going and her bare face was gorgeous in the morning light. But the look in her eyes was edgy. Determined. He could have handled that. But underneath was a hint of vulnerability that he wasn't sure what to do with.

So he let her herd him toward the door.

"I'll pick you up for dinner around six," he told her, leaning in for a kiss.

Her lips went soft and sweet under his. His hands were full, but he angled his body to trap her between him and the wall. She felt so damn good.

Then she pulled her mouth from his and slid free.

"Dinner? Um, no. I'm supposed to be getting a shipment in this evening. With the show next weekend, I'm going to be really busy."

His ego refused to believe she was giving him the brush-off. They'd been too good together. So she was afraid of something. Max narrowed his eyes. "Really busy, huh?"

She dropped her gaze and nodded. Then she flipped the locks and opened the front door. "I had a great time last night, though."

A lesser man might doubt those words in the face of the bum's rush she was giving him. But Max knew she'd enjoyed every second of their lovemaking.

"What's the deal?" he asked.

She sucked on her bottom lip. He almost groaned. Then she shrugged and gave him what he guessed was supposed to be a tough look. "I had fun, Max. A lot of fun. But you're a guaranteed distraction. I need to focus, okay? Why don't I call you when things shake loose?"

Max frowned. Her decision would give him the space to deal with his mother's mile-long to-do list, and for a little investigating into the gallery's issues. But that wouldn't take much time, especially not at night.

Still, he let her push him out the door. Then he planted one more kiss on her, watching her melt against the doorjamb.

"Pretty sure that's supposed to be my line, sweetheart," he told her, grinning as she tried to focus through the haze of desire blurring her eyes. Yeah, she might be doing the pushing, but he was the one in control. "That means I'll need to come up with a different one. I'll let you know what it is."

FIVE DAYS AND SIX VERY long, restless nights later, Sophia pressed her hand to her stomach, trying to calm the wildly dancing butterflies. Her first show as sole proprietor of Esprit de l'Art was in half an hour and she wanted to throw up.

What a week. Between trying to garner any form of publicity, and handling the caterers and the artists, she'd wondered at times if she'd pull it off. Preparation for the show had been crazy.

Just crazy enough to keep her from obsessing over Max.

Her thighs trembled, the tiny bud between them throbbing in remembered pleasure.

Every freaking time she thought of the man, her body went into a sexual meltdown. She had to get hold of herself. She rolled her eyes, remembering that getting hold of herself the night before in an attempt to relieve a little tension obviously hadn't dulled her desire.

It was a testament to her control that she'd managed to keep herself from diving for a phone and dialing Max's number.

She paced the length of her office to try to shake off a little anxiety. Show nerves, she assured herself. The simmering doubts had nothing to do with her pushing Max away.

Sure, maybe she was a little surprised that he'd backed off. After all, that'd been some pretty incredible sex, if she did say so herself. Explosively hot, orgasmically wild. And she'd offered him some toast, a bowl of fruit and a goodbye wave the next morning. She'd been afraid if she'd taken the time to scramble an egg, she'd have begged him to stay and take over her life.

But you'd think he'd have argued over his dismissal. Tried to change her mind. Maybe called a few times or dropped in to convince her to go another round of pleasure.

But had he? She barely restrained herself from kicking the couch in frustration. Nope, he'd done exactly what she wanted. Left her alone.

"The caterers are all set and the string ensemble are tuning up. You ready?" Gina asked from the doorway. Dressed in her version of conservative, black Doc Martens, a knee-length black tulle ballet skirt and a black leather corset, the other woman was bouncing on her toes.

"Sure. You okay? You seem a little nervous," Sophia said, her own anxiety tripling when she saw the unflappable Gina all on edge.

Maybe she should have worn black, too? Or in keeping with the black-and-white theme of the photographs being shown tonight, white to contrast with her assistant? She smoothed the rich red jacquard of her sheath nervously then grabbed her camera and joined the other woman in the hall. She couldn't wait to make a photo record of this evening.

"Anticipating," Gina corrected, adjusting her rhinestone-embellished glasses with a twitch of her finger. "I mean, we're shooting for a higher class of clientele tonight. Before, all I had to worry about was someone cornering me in the hallway and trying to cop a feel so he could compare me with one of the sculptures of naked lady bits."

Some of her own nerves melting in amusement, Sophia laughed.

"Oh, yeah, I had a few of those myself. Joseph always thought it was a great joke," she recalled, wrinkling her nose at the memory. Her late husband had never gone for the knight in shining armor persona. Instead he'd chide her if she was too abrupt in slapping down the idiots who hit on her. After all, he'd claimed, it was bad form to discourage sales. Not that he'd have used his wife to make a sale. He hadn't been slimy. Just oblivious.

Unlike Max, who was so hyperaware of her every mood, it was as if he was linked into her brain. She shivered as she remembered waking in the middle of the night wrapped in Max's arms, feeling sore and a little sticky. Just as the fantasy of her, Max and a bath flashed through her mind, he'd murmured a naughty suggestion that'd included bubbles, a shower massage and his tongue.

Max was anything but oblivious.

"Soph?"

Sophia forced herself to focus on now. She could obsess over Max and his magic mouth later.

"I knew how to handle the jerks and their innuendos. But this—" Gina waved her hand at the caterers arranging canapés on silver trays in the smaller showroom "—this is fancy.

These people will want to talk art. The subtleties of lighting instead of fornication. Creative vision instead of fellatio."

"Color and composition instead of methodologies of ménage a trois?" Sophia asked, snapping a picture while Gina's nervousness drained into laughter.

"Yes," Gina giggled, still bouncing. A second later, her giggles ceased and she winced. "What if I mess something up, Soph? Are you sure you wouldn't rather one of the part-timers fill in? I can keep things smooth in the background and Danny can assist tonight."

Danny was an art student and the gallery's part-time employee. "I don't need an expert tonight, Gina. I need a friend. You'll do great. Bring any technical questions to me if you have to, but I'm sure you can handle anything that comes your way."

At first Gina just stared, her eyes buggy behind those crazy glasses. Then, with a deep breath, she tucked a stray hair, orange tonight, into her black velvet headband and finally nodded.

With a deep breath of her own, and one last fleeting thought to how nice it'd be if Max were there with her, Sophia pulled back her shoulders and led the way to the front showroom.

An hour later, her nerves were a thing of the past. They'd drowned in misery and despair. She'd been right about Gina being able to handle any questions. *Where's the sexy stuff?* and *Is this crap really fish eggs?* were about the toughest queries of the night.

She'd thought she saw Max at one point, just catching a glimpse of broad shoulders and a sexy butt, but she'd obviously been mistaken. If he'd been there, he'd have said something to her.

"Danny wants to know if he should go home," Gina whispered. "I told him to wait another hour, things are bound to pick up after eight."

Sophia's shoulders slumped. Given that staff and catering

outnumbered guests four to one, cutting Danny loose was probably smart. No point paying wages when she wasn't going to be making any money.

"I don't get it," she said, not even attempting to lower her voice. Why bother? She and Gina were the only ones other than the musicians in the main showroom. "I mean, I know we didn't have much press. But still, there should be more guests. We've had this show planned for months. We sent mailings, we put an ad in the art section of the paper. We've had spur-of-the-moment, completely unpromoted shows that were better attended than this."

"Do you think it's the changes?" Gina ventured.

It took all of Sophia's willpower to keep her lower lip from drooping. She didn't want it to be. Dammit, this show was supposed to be a validation.

"I used the mailing list and contacts from when we bought the gallery. I edited our current list, targeting people who'd bought non-penis-focused art at any point. I…" She trailed off, throwing her hands in the air. Frustration wound so tight in her belly, she felt like screaming. She paced the room. "I did everything I could think of."

"Maybe you just need to accept that there's nothing else you could have done," Gina consoled.

Accept it? Wasn't it enough that she had no control over her finances, over her life, over her freaking out-of-control lusting thoughts of Max? Now she was supposed to accept that she had no control over the gallery, too?

Screw that.

Before she could dig into a full-blown temper tantrum, a large limousine pulled up to the curb out front. As if it were a flagship of some kind, another half dozen cars followed, all pulling around the side to the parking lot.

Sophia had spent her married years learning to live with money, so she had no problem recognizing it when it came waltzing through her front doors.

"Holy cannoli," Gina breathed. "It's like the cavalry just arrived decked out in diamonds and fur."

And credit cards. Sophia almost cried, she was so excited.

"Do the rounds, make sure the caterer serves fresh food and have the musicians play a little softer until everyone gets comfortable," she ordered. Shoulders back, she plastered on her most persuasive smile and strode forward to greet her rescuers.

Five minutes later, she wanted to dance through the showroom. There were at least two dozen people here now. Many she recognized as patrons who'd visited during the gallery's noneerotic heyday. Not nearly as large a crowd that attended Esprit's recent shows, but better than the single person who'd come through the previous hour.

Ten minutes later, she was more confused than giddy.

"Any interest?" she asked Gina quietly as they passed through the archway between the large and small showrooms.

"A lot of looky-loos, but no bites."

Sophia licked her lips, looked at the crowd and puffed out a breath. Then she forced herself to ask, "Are they saying anything…well, weird?"

Gina frowned.

"Compared to offers to paint my breasts in dayglo? Nope. One thing's kinda funny, though," she said slowly. "They all seem to know—"

"Max," Sophia said at the same time Gina did.

As if their duet were an incantation, he suddenly appeared in the doorway. Dressed in a dark suit, a black open-necked dress shirt and a sexy smile, he looked gorgeous.

"How'd he know we were sucking?" Gina wondered.

Maybe she really had seen him earlier. Brows furrowing, Sophia gestured for Gina to do the rounds, then strode forward to meet her questionable fairy godfather.

"Max." She'd greeted everyone else with a handshake, but she was afraid she'd melt into a puddle of lust at his touch. So she kept her hands, with her palms itching to feel him, at her sides.

"Sophia," he greeted in equal gravity, humor lurking in his dark eyes.

Despite his friendly ease, she could feel the desire pouring off him in waves. She'd never had a man want her like Max did. Never felt so feminine and sexy and wanted. It was like being in an explosion of hot need. She couldn't think of anything better than giving in to that need.

"I didn't expect to see you here," she murmured, barely aware of what she said. As long as it wasn't *Please strip naked so I can straddle your body* it probably didn't matter.

"I wanted to make sure everything came together for you."

All she heard was making sure she came. She was sure that wasn't what he'd actually said, though.

"I beg your pardon?"

"The show," he said, stepping a little closer. Sophia breathed deep his warm scent. "I wanted to be here to see a gallery show, to make sure everything went okay. And I wanted to see you and didn't figure you'd toss me out of a public event."

His smile was pure charm. His eyes were pure heat. His body, wrapped in a black suit, was pure temptation.

Then his words finally sank in.

"Why wouldn't everything go okay?" she asked, starting to frown.

As if sensing the change in her, Max tilted his head and waited. Probably all that bomb training had given him ultra-sensitive perceptive powers.

"Why do all these people seem to know you?" she asked slowly, trying to fit all the puzzle pieces together. "Did you come by earlier?"

"Don't you think I'd have said hello if I had?" he sidestepped.

She narrowed her eyes. "And these people?"

"They look like they're enjoying the photos," he mused, glancing at the people milling about. He nodded to a couple negotiating with Gina, who was bouncing on her toes again. "And buying."

"What's going on?" Sophia demanded. "Did you have anything to do with our sudden rush of patrons?"

Max gave her a long look. She'd seen that look before. It was one of those how-much-does-she-really-need-to-know looks. Her father used that look. All of her brothers used that look. Joseph hadn't even bothered with that look after the first year of their marriage.

Anger churned in Sophia's belly, masking the lust. Oh, the lust was still there. She couldn't be within five feet of Max without wanting to see him naked. But now she had an overwhelming urge to throw things at him. While he was naked.

"Actually I might have had a little to do with it. I had to escort my mother to a country club dinner this evening and mentioned the show to a few people," he explained with a shrug. "It looks like they were interested, huh?"

"You just happened to mention it?" she asked, her frown fading to a furrow between her brows.

"Yeah. I thought I'd seen a lot of their names on your mailing list when I was hanging out in your office last week," he said, grinning when she narrowed her eyes again at his admission of snooping. "I don't get why they seemed clueless about the show, but I figured you'd wanted them here and I could give them a nudge to attend."

"I sent invitations. Unless they all moved without a forwarding address, they shouldn't be clueless."

He shook his head. "Nobody I spoke with had received an invitation."

Nonplussed, she just stared. She wasn't used to men actually explaining their motivations.

The anger was still there. But now it was scattered, with no specific focus. What had happened to the invitations she'd sent, then? Was it only the high society segment of her mailing list that hadn't received them? Or everyone?

"Mrs. Castillo?"

Sophia reluctantly tore her gaze from Max's, took a deep breath and turned to face the caterer.

"Yes, Becca?" Forcing herself to focus, her frown deepened. The usually unflappable blond caterer looked as if she wanted to cry.

"Um, we have a little problem."

Sophia gave Max a look, but he didn't move away. She took Becca's arm and pulled her to the side. Max followed. She didn't bother rolling her eyes.

"What's wrong?"

"I was doing rounds with the canapés and Juliet was bringing in ice from the truck. We were doing our jobs. We weren't being lax or careless or anything," Becca insisted, blinking back tears.

Sophia's stomach slid into the toes of her pumps. "And?"

"Someone got into the food. They dumped the crackers into the shrimp, poured the chocolate syrup over the ham bites and the stuffed mushrooms are floating in the ice chest filled with all the champagne."

It took Sophia a solid five seconds to decipher her words. Since they were said in such a rush, they all tumbled over themselves.

It took her another five to blink the black mist of panic from her eyes.

"All the food?"

"And the champagne," Becca confirmed, a tear tracking down her cheek.

A quick glance confirmed that her gallery was still filled

with fancy dressed patrons with no-limit credit cards and a taste for being served champagne and shrimp.

It was all she could do not to start crying along with Becca. Sophia puffed out a breath and without thinking about it, slid her gaze to Max.

His frown was a scary thing. It was also oddly reassuring. As if it gave her permission to be pissed instead of bawling like a baby deprived of its binky.

With the anger came clear thinking. She had a gallery full of rich people whose money she wanted. To get that money, she had to make them feel relaxed and happy. Which meant feeding them.

"Becca, is there any food left in your van? Any more champagne? Or wine? Or soda even?"

"A couple bottles of champagne, a brick of cheese but no crackers, a tray of veggies and some petit fours left over from the baby shower we catered this afternoon." The blonde hesitated, then added, "We still have a box of the penis pops and some frozen soft pretzel busts from the last show."

Sophia grimaced and shook her head.

Despite growing up in the kitchen of her father's restaurant, Sophia's cooking expertise started and ended with canned soup, bagged salad and microwavable meals.

"I'll run across the street to the cantina," Max offered. "Send around the veggies, cakes and champagne while I get some appetizer trays ordered."

Becca's wince made it clear her catering menu wasn't geared toward Mexican finger food, but she nodded and hurried out of the room.

Torn between independence and the need to salvage the evening, Sophia hesitated. Then, realizing she was being an idiot, she laid her hand on his arm. "Thank you."

His smile was slow and melting. He lifted her hand, brushed a kiss over her knuckles and murmured, "You can thank me later."

Oh, baby! It took her thirty seconds to catch her breath and force her legs to move. She did her hostess gig, charming her way through the crowd and enjoying every second of what was—thanks to Max—shaping up to be a fabulous show. Within a quarter of an hour, Becca's staff was circulating with appetizers—because really, nobody could call empanadas an hors d'oeuvre—trays. Sophia watched anxiously, but everyone who tried it seemed to enjoy the food.

And then Max was back at her side and the last of her tension seeped from her shoulders and spine.

"Hi," she murmured, smiling up at him. "Do you do this knight-in-shining-armor role very often?"

"Do you like it?" he asked softly, reaching out to rub his index finger over her shoulder. Such a simple move melted her insides.

"Sophia?"

She reluctantly pulled her gaze from Max's. "Yes, Danny?"

"There's a customer who'd like to speak with you about the Redwood series."

"I'll be right there." She looked back at Max, relieved to see him already nodding.

"Go make a sale," he said. "I'll work the room."

Grateful for his help and his support, she smiled. Then, knowing what she was offering, she stepped closer and brushed her lips, just a tiny kiss, against his. "Thanks."

Sophia was halfway to the hall when she heard the scream.

A bony, lace-encased woman wearing enough diamonds to buy a small country screamed again, falling onto the velvet settee and drawing her knees up to her chest.

Sophia ran forward, Max right beside her. Gina came scurrying toward them, one hand holding a sales receipt, her other covering her mouth and nose.

Before they could ask her what happened, the room gushed

people. They just sort of poured out, hands over mouths and nose as they rushed for the door.

The front door. Escaping.

"No," Sophia moaned, reaching out as if she could grab them all back. Or at least their credit cards.

Shoulders sagging, she arched a brow at Gina.

"Skunk" was Gina's muffled response.

Sophia would have dropped to the floor if Max hadn't leaned in and wrapped his arm around her shoulders.

"How the hell…"

Max's growl worked as well as if he'd taken her by the shoulders and shaken her. Sophia battled back the panic, sucked in a breath and tried to remember the rules of control. She was pretty sure *do something* was somewhere on the list.

"Gina, see if anyone's left in the gallery and, if so, try and charm them into buying something."

"What're you going to do?" Gina mumbled from behind her hand.

Sophia wrinkled her nose. "The skunk didn't spray, did it? I don't smell anything."

"Not yet."

"Then I'm going to get it out before it does something to ruin the upholstery."

"I can take care of this, Sophia," Max offered, his hand on her shoulder as if he was trying to steer her in the opposite direction as the skunk.

"It's my gallery," was all Sophia said.

As she'd expected, Max stayed at her side as they crossed under the arch and into the smaller showroom. Despite her expectations, though, he didn't try to push her aside and take over.

He didn't have to. She skidded to a halt in the doorway.

It was a disaster. Broken champagne glasses, food all over

the floor, one of the huge ficus plants overturned and dirt scattered everywhere.

Sitting there, in the middle of her red plush velvet settee with rosewood trim was a very large skunk, eating a canapé.

"Shit," Max breathed, taking in the mess with a quick look before wrapping one arm around her and pulling her close. His arms were safe, secure. She turned into him. His chest a warm haven.

The sweet move almost melted her heart.

For just a second, Sophia let herself be weak. She let him hold her, drew in his strength as if it had healing powers.

All she wanted to do was lean in. To let him take over. Obviously she was doing a lousy job of things, so why not hand over the reins.

"Soph?"

Defeated, Sophia glanced around Max's shoulder with dull eyes.

"Everybody left," Gina said quietly. "I called animal control to pick up the skunk."

"I need a break," Sophia murmured, pulling out of Max's arms. She instantly wanted to burrow back again and hide.

She glanced at the mess again and winced. Yeah, she definitely needed a break. Maybe a long one.

Shaking her head at Gina's questioning look, she slowly made her way back to her office and shut the door. She didn't even have the energy to turn the lock. Instead, the two steps feeling like two miles, she walked over to the couch and collapsed.

God, what a disaster.

MAX FINISHED HIS INSPECTION of the gallery. He'd talked to everyone, from the catering crew to Gina to the crowd at the cantina across the street to see if anyone had seen anything. Nada.

He checked with Jorge, the cantina busboy he'd hired last Wednesday to watch the gallery when he couldn't. Jorge had seen a motorcycle drive by and pause in front of the gallery, but it hadn't parked. Max remembered seeing a motorcycle the day he'd first met Sophia, the day the gallery had been trashed. He'd bet it was the same bike.

But other than Danny, who'd seen a guy with dark hair dressed in a catering jacket—in contrast to Becca's assistants, who were all women—there wasn't much else to go on.

He didn't need much to know that this was a personal vendetta against Sophia, though. And he was going to make sure whatever it was stopped.

But first he had to make sure Sophia was okay. He headed for her office. A year of watching untold degrees of pain, suffering and misery had molded a hard shell around his heart. He needed that shell. And damn if he didn't feel it melting away a little at the sight of her sitting at her desk. With her head in her hands and the luxurious curtain of silky black hair falling over her face, she looked defeated.

"Sophia?" he said quietly, afraid if he crossed the threshold he'd push her over the edge.

She shifted so her fists supported her chin instead of her forehead. Her eyes drooped a little at the sides, matching the heaviness of her mouth. It physically hurt to see her so unhappy.

He wanted to take care of her. He wanted to wrap her in his arms, tuck her away someplace quiet and fix this mess so she could get back to making her dream come true.

Rico would have applauded that idea. Hell, he'd practically said as much in the email Max had received that morning.

Sophia's independent streak is a PITA, amigo. It's easier to work around her, keep her distracted while you do the heavy lifting. She's not much muscle-wise and needs someone to take care of her.

Max was pretty sure that Sophia would take her not-much muscles and use them to kick her brother's ass if she ever read that email.

And his if he tried that kind of crap on her. So instead of doing the end run he'd prefer, Max steeled his heart and forced himself to add to her stress load.

"The cops are here," he said.

"Can you deal with them?" she asked quietly. "I'm really not up to it."

He almost turned heel to do just that, then stopped. She'd damn near ripped his head off when he'd tried to deal with her business last week. He thought of Rico's note again and with a sigh shook his head.

"It's your place," he told her. "You're the one in charge. Not me."

Her shrug said she didn't give a damn.

Max's frown intensified.

"You're not going to let them win, are you?" he asked quietly, needing to see something out of her besides defeat. God, where was her anger, her fighting spirit? She couldn't have used it all up on him.

"Them?"

"Someone's screwing with you. Deliberately trying to run you out of business." He glanced around the office, inwardly winced because he knew he was risking the best sex he'd ever had, and said, "Are you going to give up on the gallery the same as you bailed on your photography? Don't you have any guts? Or are you, what's the term Rico uses? *El pollo loco?*"

Her eyes narrowed.

"A crazy chicken? You think I'm bailing?" Her voice hitched. "You think just because my big brother appointed you my protector, suddenly you're the expert on my life?"

"Nope." He tucked his hands in his pockets and rocked back on his heels, forcing himself not to smile. "I'm the guy who thought you were a savvy businesswoman who knew what she wanted and had a plan to get it. But then, maybe I was wrong."

Her jaw worked. Her eyes sizzled. Lust speared through Max like lightning. He wondered how long they had before the cops came back here looking for her. Probably not long enough for what his body was craving.

She shoved away from the desk so hard her chair hit the wall. Fists clenched at the sides of her pretty red dress, she stomped around the desk.

Definitely not enough time to soothe her out of her tantrum. He was treading on thin ice but he couldn't stop his grin.

"I'll deal with you later," she said with a glare as she swept around him, all princess to peasant. "After I've spoken with the police."

"I can't wait," he murmured, watching the delicious swing of her hips as she stormed off. Then he rescued her chair and settled in behind her desk.

But he was the one who'd be dealing. Only it'd be some comfort and soothing. And, once Sophia was feeling less stressed and upset, maybe they could find other ways to relax.

Max thought of the bag he'd left in the backseat of his car. Bubble bath, candles, the docking station for his iPod. All he needed to set a soothing scene.

And in the meantime? Time to do a little investigating. Starting by poking through the gallery's files.

9

HER BODY WARM, LAX AND well-loved, Sophia slowly made her way to the surface of consciousness. She tingled all over. While she was finishing with the police, Max had talked Gina into letting him into her apartment, where he had filled her bathroom with candlelight, music and hot, frothy bubbles. Then he'd seduced her into forgetting all her woes.

Eyes still closed, she sighed and stretched. She didn't get far. Her toes skimmed a hair-dusted leg and her butt wiggled against a very hard male body.

She gave a sleepy frown, her fingers tracing the arm that lay across her waist. The hand at the end of that arm slid up, cupping the heavy warmth of her breast.

Her frown faded as the fingers worked magic on the tip of her breast. Swirling, tweaking, flicking. She gasped. Heat swept down her body, pooling wet and sticky between her legs.

She shifted her hips, smiling at the hard length of desire pressing against her. She wasn't the only one feeling the love here.

Her hair was swept aside.

She clenched her thighs, all her girly bits trembling at the sensation. Who knew the back of the neck was an erogenous zone? Then again, who knew there was a direct line to her G-spot when Max touched her?

"Mmm, I feel good," she said in a sleepy murmur. She loved what he was doing, but needed more. She wanted to play, too. Sophia turned in his arms, giving Max a warm smile and practically purred. "I really like your plan for working off stress."

"Bottled-up stress is a health hazard," Max assured her, his mouth tracing whisper soft kisses along her jaw and down the sensitive skin of her throat. "You need to release it before it causes problems."

"You definitely offered a lot of releases last night," she said with a breathless laugh.

"You up for another?" he asked. His smile said sex, but his sleep-rumpled cuteness made her want to hug him close and giggle. He was just…amazing.

His mouth moved lower so his soft kisses were now focused on the tips of her breast. She heard the rustle of foil, then felt his fingers warm between her legs. Testing, teasing, readying her for the ride.

Before she could do more than sigh with pleasure, he slid into her. Gentle and sweet, just like the kisses warming her throat. Sophia's breath shuddered as they rocked together. Max shifted so his eyes could hold hers. She wanted to blink, to look away, but knew he'd stop the delicious dance if she did. While he'd happily do anything, absolutely anything, she wanted, Max insisted on real intimacy with their lovemaking. It added a scary layer of tenderness and honesty to the passion.

He shifted higher. She wrapped her legs around his waist, resting her weight on her arms as he rose to his knees and stared down at her body. For a brief second, he dropped his eyes to watch their bodies slide together. Sophia followed his gaze. Four years of erotic exposure had taught her that she was a bit of a prude, so she expected to have to hide her ick reaction. Instead, though, the sight of their bodies joining made her gasp.

Sexy, hot, intense. Her heart pounded. Passion intensified. Her eyes met Max's again. His hands gripped the soft flesh of her butt, holding her in place as he pumped, in and out. The heat intensified, swirling tighter. Her body tensed. His eyes darkened.

She panted, her entire being focused on reaching higher. Climbing. Grasping. Her eyes glazed, her brain shut off as her body took over. Max plunged. Sophia exploded.

The climax was so strong, so wild, it shook her whole body. She shuddered, her thighs squeezing tight. Max tensed. She forced her eyes open, needing to see him fall over the edge. Deeper. Harder. Over and over. Then, his head thrown back, he came with a loud growl of delight. His climax sent Sophia over the edge once again.

Oh, yeah. He was definitely amazing.

Ten minutes later, sated and starving, Sophia wrapped herself in one of the blankets they'd kicked to the floor and headed for the kitchen.

"Toast, dry cereal or toaster waffles?" she asked as she skirted around the short counter that separated the kitchen from the rest of the apartment.

"Breakfast of Champions," he teased.

Her shoulders tightened and her stomach tightened. Self-doubts she'd worked hard to overcome suddenly wagged their judging fingers. She should have good food to offer a guest. She should have man food. She should know how to cook it, or at least have thought to get up and have it delivered.

An apology on her lips, Sophia glanced back at Max, who hadn't bothered with a blanket, but lounged on the bed, half sitting with his arms behind his head and with a look of total satisfaction on his face.

That was not a man who was looking for an apology. Unable to help herself, she grabbed her camera off the counter and snapped a picture before Max could react.

"I also have fat-free yogurt, a spotty banana and some leftover chocolate cake," she offered with a grin.

He gave a good-natured grimace.

"Sweetheart, I spent the past year on MREs—meals ready-to-eat. I'm not picky. If you want a fancy breakfast, we can get dressed and I'll take you out," he offered. "Or we can stay naked and lick toast crumbs off each other. Totally your call."

She wordlessly dropped bread in the toaster. Then, feeling adventurous—who wouldn't after eight, count 'em, baby, orgasms and a whole new understanding of the number sixty-nine—she scooped yogurt into two bowls and sliced the banana over them. She opened the cupboard and pulled out a can of almonds and sprinkled a few over the bananas.

"This'd probably be better if I'd chopped the almonds," she told Max as she loaded the bowls and toasted bread onto the tray she usually ate dinner on. "But I don't have a sharp knife."

He shifted so she could set the tray in the middle of the bed. "Can I ask a personal question?" he asked around a mouthful of toast.

"You had me bent over the bathroom sink last night," Sophia teased, spooning up some yogurt. "I think we're way beyond personal, don't you think?"

"Why do you live so spartanly? You have a low-end apartment furnished with less than most college kids move out with, and a ten-year-old car."

Her teasing smile fell away. Sophia looked around the apartment. It wasn't as luxurious as the estate in which she'd spent her married life, or as comfortable as the home she'd grown up in. But it was hers. Her very first place of her own.

"I like it here," she said, her tone a little defensive.

He just arched a brow.

"And it's all I can afford," she admitted. There was no shame in being poor, Sophia knew. She'd grown up borderline poor. The cantina and raising seven kids had gobbled up every penny her father made.

"I thought Castillo was pretty well off," Max asked with a frown. "And the gallery isn't chump change."

He winced after he'd asked, as if he was a little worried he'd stepped over a line. Sophia considered that for a second. He'd seen her naked. He'd had her every way there was, at least in her limited knowledge, to have a body. He'd held her after the nightmare that was supposed to be a showing at the gallery. And he'd let her call all the shots the previous night, from talking to the cops to handling the help to who cleaned up what. He understood her enough to know she needed that. A man had to really, *really* care to understand a woman that well.

Nope. No lines between them.

"Joseph's daughter contested the will. She's laid claim to everything except the gallery, which is in my name outright."

"And you let her?" he asked incredulously.

Maybe there were lines after all. Sophia lifted her chin and tightened the blanket, suddenly very aware and very irritated by her nakedness.

"It's not so much a matter of letting her as not being able to stop her."

He frowned, sliding from the bed to tug on his jeans, commando-style, and carried the tray across to the kitchen counter. Her mouth drooled. She'd just seen him in his full glory and the sight of the man in unzipped jeans and a bare chest made her wish she knew what really kinky sex was so she could do it to him.

It took her a few seconds to realize he'd returned to the side of the bed and was staring at her, one brow raised and a questioning look on his face.

"I take it you don't get along with your stepdaughter?"

"Not even a little bit."

"Did you ever consider that she might be the one behind all of your problems?"

Sophia rolled her eyes. "Are you trying to piss me off?"

Max stared for a second, then nodded. "Of course you've considered it."

"Lynn is an indulged, selfish, spoiled brat with major entitlement issues. But she's also very confident that she'll win the lawsuit. Why would she bother to mess with the gallery?"

"Maybe to hurt you?"

Sophia shrugged. "Lynn wouldn't think twice about trying to hurt me. And ruin the gallery? She'd love nothing more."

"Have you told the police?"

"The police. My lawyer. Gina," Sophia confirmed. "But suspecting, even wanting, it to be her doesn't make it fact. As far as I know, as anyone knows, she hasn't done anything."

"This is why you should have hired the P.I.'s," Max murmured.

Sophia clenched her jaw. Then Max smoothed his hand along her shoulder. Down her arm, then back up, so his fingers brushed the insides of her breast where the sheet didn't cover them.

Irritation at his suggestion melted under the onslaught of lust. She sighed.

"I can't afford to hire an investigator," she admitted. "Maybe, if last night's show had done well, I could have considered it. But now? It's out of the question."

She tensed a little, waiting for him to offer money or some other humiliating resolution to her woes. She couldn't accept, and he'd argue and push, then they'd fight. Then everything would be ruined. She had to force herself not to climb off the bed and prepare to stand her ground.

"Have you considered a compromise?" he asked absently,

his eyes focused on her body and the amount of skin he was systematically revealing with his sneaky fingers.

That wasn't an offer. Nor was it pushy. She blinked a couple of times, trying to figure out what he was up to.

But she couldn't think when he was touching her like that.

"Huh?" she asked, barely following his words now that the sheet had been teased aside to expose one breast. He was barely touching her, his finger a whisper. But his eyes caressed, enticed. Wet heat pooled between her legs and she swallowed hard.

"Compromise," he said, leaning forward to blow gently, making her nipple pucker in response. "You want the gallery to focus on photographs. The kink drew a big audience and made money. Show erotic photos."

"Like von Schilling's?" she murmured, her breath coming in short little pants.

"The guy sounded like he really wanted to show here," Max pointed out. He flicked her nipple with his tongue, making desire spear through her body like lightning.

"No," she said, lying back and drawing him with her. She held his head to her breast, loving the feeling of his mouth working her nipple. She wrapped one leg around his thigh, the abrasive feel of denim against her swollen bud making her whimper. "That'd be a step backward."

Max skimmed his hand beneath the sheet, teasing little trails of fire everywhere he touched. His fingers dipped into her wet heat, soothing and enticing with each stroke.

He shifted his weight, sucking her other nipple through the sheet, the wet fabric adding another layer of delight. Then he slid down, his breath sending shivers through her as he skimmed his tongue along her torso and belly.

"Compromise, sweetheart. Sometimes you gotta pull out a little before you drive it home," he said before he settled between her legs and took her into his mouth and exploded all thoughts of the gallery into tiny pieces.

"I STILL THINK YOU SHOULD call von Schilling," Max advised for the hundredth time as he pulled into his mother's driveway.

He and Sophia had spent the past week together, in and out of bed. The in-bed Sophia was great. She was amazing. Sweet, sexy and adventurous. The out-of-bed woman was a little more challenging. She was smart, sexy and adventurous there, too. But unlike in bed, she wasn't willing to let him be on top.

Ever.

It was enough to give a guy a complex.

The only thing—besides the incredible sex—keeping his ego propped up was playing secret investigator when Sophia wasn't paying attention. He hadn't found anything, but he was pretty sure he'd tapped the vandal. He hadn't made the guy's face, but that motorcycle had been back three times, its license plate covered in mud. He'd slow down, notice Max, then speed off.

"And I think we should have a naked lunch at my apartment," Sophia decided after a quick glance at the fancy-ass Nob Hill property. Max wasn't sure, but he thought she gave a little shudder. Probably she wasn't comfy with the snobby upper crust. He could relate.

"How about naked dessert?" he compromised, offering his most charming smile. His ego, among other things, swelled a little when she got that dazed do-me look in her eyes.

"I can't do naked dessert if lunch gives me a nervous stomach," Sophia warned, her smile a little shaky. "I shouldn't have taken the afternoon off, anyway. The gallery needs me."

"I need you," Max said as he reached over and took her hand, lifting it to his mouth and brushing a kiss over her softly scented, silky skin. "And I already told you, pull in von Schilling, a couple other photographers that specialize in sexy and do a show. Voilà, all your problems are solved."

When she tugged her hands from his and offered an impatient roll of her pretty blue eyes, Max briefly wished he were back in Afghanistan where people actually obeyed his orders without question or argument.

"I told you, it's in the gallery's best interest that I stick with the plan," she said for the hundredth time. What she'd never explained, though, was *why* it was in the gallery's best interest. "Now change the subject, please and tell me why I have to have lunch with you."

"You're here to protect me," he said, only partially teasing.

"I'm here to protect the big bad bomb defuser from his mama?"

Max grinned, flicking off the engine and leaning over to give her a kiss. "Exactly."

Her smile faded as fast as it came. He recognized the look on her face when she glanced at the house. Dread.

"What's wrong? You lived in similar overblown luxury when you were married, right?" he teased, wanting—needing—to put her at ease. After all, things would be tense enough inside. No point in her being all stressed out before the soup course.

"I did, but as I was often reminded, I never quite fit in," she said with a one-shouldered shrug and a half smile.

Not for the first time, Max wished her ex-husband had lived long enough for her to divorce him. Then he'd still be around to get his sorry ass kicked like he deserved. Over the course of the past week, Sophia had told him enough—and not told him even more—to let him know that the old guy had been a first-class jerk, emotionally abusive and totally unappreciative.

When he'd asked Sophia why she'd married him, she'd given this sad sort of smile and said he was her Prince Charming.

Whatever the hell that meant.

"I probably should have warned you," he started. "My family is…difficult."

"I have six overprotective brothers and a hardheaded father. You don't think I can handle this?" she asked, one brow arched. The look in her beautiful blue eyes was both confident and vulnerable.

Max didn't know how to answer. He wasn't even sure he could handle this. But it was the only way to stem the flow of his mother's nagging him to date Tabby-approved women. Under normal circumstances, his mother was interfering and pushy, but she still loved her son and wanted him to be happy. Lately, though, she'd been antsy and snappy. She was obsessed with her historical society vendetta against that building.

He glanced at the wide doors and had his hand on the ignition key before he realized it.

"Running away?" Sophia asked. Her words were teasing, but her look was hopeful.

He really wanted to.

But years of training, from both the military and his family—not that there was really much difference—came to the forefront. Max sighed, then offered her a smile as he pulled the keys from the steering column and opened the driver's door.

He was around the car and opening Sophia's door before she'd gathered her purse.

"Remember this morning?" he asked as she took his hand to exit the car.

An appealing blush washed her cheeks and she gave him a questioning glance. "You mean this morning on my desk?"

"Exactly." He tucked her hand into the crook of his and held it there, as much to force himself up the stairs as to keep her from running. "If you stick it out through this meal, I promise that again for dessert."

Her eyes glowed with wicked amusement and her mouth

made an oh. Before she could respond, though, Sterling opened the door.

"Sergeant," the butler greeted.

Max greeted the older man with a smile, noting the questioning look Sophia slanted his way. He probably should have warned her that while it looked like a home, in reality they were eating at a very fancy, very upscale military base.

He could only hope the brass skipped this particular meal.

"Your mother and uncle are entertaining the rest of the guests in the parlor," Sterling instructed.

So much for that wish. God, he hoped his mother and uncle didn't act like snobs with Sophia. They were so obsessed with status and connections, sometimes they could come off as... well, as assholes if they didn't think someone measured up.

As usual, though, Max kept his feelings to himself and, taking Sophia's hand in his, drew her down the hallway.

Thirty minutes later, they all sat down to eat. Max assured himself that the afternoon wasn't any different than approaching a live bomb with a civilian to protect.

He was courageous, skilled and unwavering in his determination to defuse the potential explosion.

Which meant they had an eighty-percent chance of survival.

"I'm sorry the Gaskins and the Lorimars couldn't stay to eat," Tabby said as she took her seat and waved a hand at Sterling to begin serving. "They are off to the Museum of Modern Art for the afternoon. I think it'd be fun to join them at the ballet this evening, though, don't you?"

"Waste of time," the General muttered as he stabbed a forkful of the salad that'd just been set in front of him. "Ballet is second only to opera in things I'd rather be shot than do."

Silently echoing an agreement, Max noticed Sophia pressing her lips together to keep from smiling.

"But you like art, right, General?" Max prodded. He

figured the old man could be an ally in his campaign to save Sophia's business. If Max played it right, the General would do all the convincing he, himself, hadn't been able to.

"Some art can be good."

"Photography?"

"Pictures are better than that crap they call art. Twisted metal, splashes of paint on a wall. Who comes up with that crap?"

Sophia had said very little all afternoon, mostly smiling, nodding and staying unobtrusive. He saw her fingers twitch a few times, though. The same way they often did right before she grabbed a camera. He wondered if it was artistic curiosity or simply a defense mechanism.

"Weren't you and Dad pretty tight with a photographer once upon a time?" Max asked his mom. He knew the answer already, but the game had to be played the right way if he was going to win.

"No," Tabby snapped. Everyone stopped eating to stare. Max frowned as a hint of color seeped into his mother's face, but before he could figure out what'd bothered her, the General cleared his throat.

"Marshall and I knew one," he offered, frowning at the past as if he were trying to gather the memory together. "Not sure if Tabby here ever met him, though. Van something."

Max's mother opened her mouth as if to correct her brother-in-law, then closed it and viciously stabbed a piece of arugula. Sophia frowned, giving Max an arch look. Confused by the undercurrents, but still undaunted, he sipped his lemon water and smiled.

"Right," Max said. "I remember Dad buying a few of his photos. Aren't they hanging in the library or something?"

Max wasn't sure why his mother was glaring at her plate. Sophia's glare was easy to understand, though. And it didn't bode well for his naked dessert plans.

Maybe it was time to change the subject. Before he could,

though, his uncle leaned back from his empty plate so it could be cleared and tapped his fingers on the table.

"If I recall, he was pretty damn famous," the General mused. "Eccentric, too. Those artist types always are. He sold pictures all over the world, traveled more than I did in my first tour of duty, and refused to show at any place except this obscure little hole in the wall here in the city. I went to a few shows with Marshall. He was a...what do you call it, Tabby? Patron or something."

Sophia's frown had faded. She smiled her thanks when Sterling cleared her plate and asked, "He didn't show anywhere else? I'd think with that level of fame, he could command top showings anywhere in the country."

"Right, he could," the General agreed, his gaze fixed on his plate as he carved into his steak. "He had a thing with the owner. Signed a lifelong exclusive."

"Lifelong?" Sophia asked. "Doesn't that mean as long as the owner has the gallery?"

"Nah. As long as the picture place is still at that location." The General laughed, shaking his head. "Guy must've signed that contract in the seventies. All that free love and freer dope got to him, if you ask me. Nothing a stint in the service wouldn't have fixed. But he never served."

Sophia leaned forward, obviously surprised at the news of the exclusive. "This photographer, is it von Schilling by any chance?"

The General shrugged, scooping up some potatoes. "Something like that. Marshall paid more attention than I did. He was stationed here at the time. I was over in Germany."

Max could see Sophia's mind working. Obviously she'd never seen this contract, but it could only work in her favor. He made a mental note to tell her to push for a higher commission since they had von Schilling in a corner.

Obviously finished with the polite chit chat, the General turned his attention toward Max. "Now, I've got some good news, Sergeant. I've made a few calls, pulled a few strings. I've found a stateside post for you. One with enough prestige and potential to set you up quite nicely."

Sophia's eyes rounded, her gaze bouncing between the two men while Max's mother continued to silently eat her salad-only lunch.

"Perhaps this is something we should discuss later," Max suggested, amusement fading as his almost-victory began to fizzle. Irritation surged at the interference, well-meaning though he knew it was.

"This post won't be open for long, Max. We need to get the orders written, get things moving immediately."

"We have a guest," Max pointed out tightly.

"Charles, this isn't the time."

Sophia's gaze bounced around the table.

"Bull pucky," the General said with a hearty laugh, waving away both Max and his mother's protest. "If the girl is interested in you, she'd be glad to hear you're sticking around."

"My leave is up in two weeks," Max said, his tone calm.

"Which is why we need to get you reassigned right away."

"I don't want to be reassigned," Max stated, leaning forward and staring straight at his uncle.

"You'd question orders?"

"I'd question nepotistic interference in my career," Max said, at attention even though he was seated. Familiar frustration pounded through him. All of his training meant he took orders from his superiors. He accepted that in the field. When he was on duty, he never questioned a command, no matter how much he might personally disagree. But here? At his mother's table? Because his uncle was brass and wearing his freaking uniform, Max was expected to silently follow along.

"It's my job to oversee your career."

"No, sir," Max denied, using every bit of control at his

disposal to keep his tone level and emotionless. "I'm not under your direct command. I appreciate your advice, but I prefer to stay where I'm currently stationed."

Max's uncle sat stock-still, his stare a lethal weapon. Max felt Sophia's tension radiating off her like a heat wave. His mother, used to these skirmishes at mealtimes, signaled Sterling to bring her a drink.

Regret washed over him for bringing Sophia into this mess. He reached under the table to take her hand and squeeze it in silent apology.

Before he could let go, he felt her take a deep breath. Out of the corner of his eye he caught the movement as she knocked her ice water across the table.

"Oh, my gosh," she exclaimed, jumping up and shaking the fabric of her now soaked skirt. "I'm so sorry. I'm a total klutz, obviously."

Tabby jumped up, using her napkin to try and stem the pool of water. The General rolled his eyes. Max's lips twitched.

Before anyone could say anything, though, she continued. "I hate to be a bother, but I'm going to be miserably uncomfortable in this wet dress. Would you all mind terribly if Max rushes me home?"

His uncle's frown was rivaled only by the patent relief on Tabby's face. Sophia continued to babble apologies and thanks all the way out of the room, glancing back only once to make sure Max was following.

By the time they reached his car, Max's grin was full-fledged and he was laughing out loud.

"Subtle," he complimented her as she slid into the passenger seat.

"Hey," she said when he took his place behind the steering wheel, "now can we focus on what really matters? Didn't you promise me a naked dessert?"

10

FLIPPING THROUGH THE MAIL, Sophia tried to remember the blissful pleasure she'd woken up to, with Max doing naughtily delicious things to her body. But with each envelope, her mood sank deeper.

Bill, bill, bill, letter from Rico, bill, letter from her attorney, bill.

This sucked. She'd rather be back at Max's mother's being treated like a hooker with open sores. Between Tabby—and what the hell kind of name was that?—and her horrified chilly looks, and the General—what the hell kind of name was that, did the man sleep with his combat boots on?—and his overbearing attitude, that had definitely been the most miserable lunch she'd ever experienced. And to discover von Schilling had an exclusive contract with Esprit? Now that had been a shock.

And still it'd be preferable to this morning.

She might as well face it. The gallery was sinking fast. The most exciting thing that'd happened at her big show was a skunk attending. She'd sold nothing in the past week. Artists were pulling their work.

At this rate, she'd lose the gallery before summer.

She sank into her desk chair and threw the mail, half of

it unread, onto her desk so it scattered in an angry fan of envelopes. The movement jostled her computer mouse, pulling her computer out of hibernation.

On the screen, mocking her, was her goals chart. Bright colored rectangles, each filled with an unachieved goal.

At least she could highlight the purple box with its dream of having a fabulous and fulfilling sex life. Who knew, the one goal she'd been sure was a pipedream was the only one she'd achieve.

No wonderful career. No returning the gallery to its former glory. No proving she was savvy, strong and in control. The only time she was on top these days was when she had Max stretched out beneath her.

Too bad finally finding the key to great sex couldn't solve all the rest of her problems.

Heart heavy and confidence skimming the floor, Sophia found her fingers moving of their own volition. They slid the mouse arrow over to the photo file and opened the pictures she'd taken of Max. Other than highlighting them in the upload box on her computer, she hadn't once looked at them. What was the point?

Pictures were windows to the soul. A snapshot of the inner self. Without the force of his commanding—albeit charming—personality, she'd see what was underneath all that sexy sizzle. It'd be one of two things.

She'd either see that he wasn't what she thought—and she'd be heartbroken—

Or she'd see that he was everything she'd ever dreamed of—and she'd be terrified.

Because Max wasn't sticking around.

Oh, sure, at first his being a sexy soldier boy who'd be heading back overseas had been one of the things in his favor. After a lifetime of men bossing her around, the idea of having one who had a defined deadline, who'd head back to his job defusing bombs and saving the world, held a lot of appeal. There was a freedom in opening her life, her body, to a man like that.

The plan had been to have a great time, with the built-in relationship deadline keeping her from opening her heart.

She poked her finger at the ugly splay of envelopes on her desk and sneered. Apparently all of her plans equally sucked.

Still…

Her heart pounded a heavy beat in her chest, so loud she could feel it all the way to the tips of her hair. No matter, she had to look.

Two quick clicks and she'd pulled up the slideshow of Max's pictures. The first one had her laughing aloud. There he was, hot and sexy soldier boy, wrapped around a marble cock almost as tall as he was. His muscles bulged beneath the cotton of his shirt. Muscles she had since spent delightful hours stroking and enjoying. Sophia clicked the plus key and zoomed in on Max's face. Sexy, focused on lifting the heavy marble. His mouth was set. His jaw determined. She zoomed in more, and there, his eyes laughed. Amused delight, both at the situation, at Sophia and at himself.

She smiled a little. For such a driven man, Max always seemed to find a way to enjoy himself.

She clicked through a few more pictures, stopping at one where Max was naked. The shot was only his head and shoulders, but since he'd been spread out on her sheets, she knew he'd been completely bare right down to his sexy toes. The look on his face made her thighs tremble.

Pure sex. Those amused eyes promised a good time. The half smile had a satisfied tilt to it, speaking well of the intense passion they'd shared right before she'd grabbed her camera.

Sophia zoomed in on Max's face and tried to push past the desire and focus on what she saw.

Honesty. Pride. Intelligence. Amusement and desire. A hint of stubborn determination.

And love.

Her eyes burned. She pressed her lips together, and, trying to focus, blinked away the moisture.

He hadn't said anything about love. He'd barely said anything about like. They didn't talk about those things. No mention of a relationship, no hint of the future. Max wasn't going to make promises, and he definitely wasn't going to corner her into making any.

Which was exactly what she wanted.

And yet…there was that love. Real, intense, accepting. She stood toe to toe with him, sometimes arguing just for the sake of proving she had a spine, and he didn't leave. He just watched, sometimes he yelled back, always he helped her defuse. And he still cared.

He tried to point out a smarter way to do business, and she ignored him. He suggested ways for her to fight for her inheritance, and she told him to mind his own business. He took her to meet his family, and she dumped water on the priceless furnishings. He listened to her plans for the future, her pie-in-the-sky hopes for the gallery. He'd even coaxed out of her the deep, hidden dream of being a professional photographer.

All the while, he wore that charming smile and made her feel great about herself. He might have rolled his eyes and stalked off a few times when she refused to listen, but he'd never made her feel stupid. Never, ever made her feel less than capable, less than in full control.

Except, of course, in bed. There he'd taught her that giving up control brought both of them more pleasure.

No man in her life had ever looked at her, really looked at the real her, and accepted what they saw.

"Soph?"

She swiped a tear from her cheek and looked at the doorway. Gina, in her ripped stovepipe jeans and Metallica T-shirt, stood with a worried look on her face.

"What's up?" Sophia asked. That it would be something bad was inevitable. Everything lately had been bad. At least, when it came to the gallery.

"Special delivery."

"Another penis?"

Looking like she didn't know whether she should give Sophia a hug, run out for chocolate or ignore the tears, Gina finally settled for a grin. "I wish. Nope. A letter. It looks legal."

Sophia's stomach jittered. "Lynn must be upping the game."

"Maybe it's time to kick her where it hurts?" Gina said, unconsciously echoing Max's argument.

"She can afford harder boots than I can," Sophia said. It wasn't defeat, she told herself. She wasn't being a wimp by not fighting. She was choosing her priorities and ensuring she achieved them. That was control. Not cowardice.

And maybe if she recited that a few million times, she'd actually believe it. Because obviously she wasn't doing much of a job at convincing anyone else.

A case in point was standing in front of her. Gina opened her mouth to argue, then gave a grimace that reached all the way to her eyes, half-hidden behind the huge seventies-style, bug-eyed glasses she wore today. Then she set the eight-by-ten envelope on Sophia's desk.

"Lynn may have harder boots, but you have a better aim," Gina replied.

Sophia could see the frustration in the other woman's eyes.

She knew Gina, like Max, wanted her to find a way to fight Lynn. They didn't care that Olivia, Sophia's lawyer, was adamant that the gallery—and Sophia—stay away from anything controversial. Especially with the settlement conference coming up in a week. Olivia had just argued two days before that as long as Sophia stayed the course, she was proving all those rumors false, which would go over well with the judge.

It was as if her hands were tied. Yes, she supposedly finally had control over her own life. But she couldn't use it.

"I'm running across the street to get lunch," Gina told her. "Want to watch the front or should I lock the door?"

A month ago, neither of them would have considered locking the door. But after all the vandalism and problems, it was now second-nature.

"I'll come out," Sophia said. She skirted the desk, ignoring the envelope. The lousy news would still be there after she'd had her chili relleno.

"WHAT THE FUCK?"

Max glared at the letter. He wanted to wad it into a ball and throw it across the room. He wanted to rip it to shreds and stomp it into the cement floor. Even better, he wanted to punch the man responsible for it in the face.

Years of military training kept him in check, though.

He sucked in a breath, then met the eyes of the man behind the desk in front of him. The man who'd had the unfortunate task of delivering the letter. Apparently some things, while not better, still demanded that personal touch.

"Colonel, I'd like to formally protest this reassignment," he said, the letter at his side now as he stood at attention. He wasn't in uniform. He wasn't on duty. It didn't matter. He was a soldier in the presence of his superior.

"St. James, I understand your frustration. Truth be told, I don't want to lose you from EOD. You're a fine leader. You're a credit to your squad, to your company and to your family's history of service."

"Permission to speak freely, sir?"

"Permission granted."

Max relaxed into parade rest and looked at the man sitting behind the beat-up metal desk. The Oakland Army Base didn't lend itself to fancy or frills. Neither did Colonel Gilden. Like most brass in the area, Max knew the older man through his father and uncle. He also knew the guy was honest, by the book and known for doing whatever it took to take care of his men.

Max wondered how far that'd go.

"Sir, my uncle is pulling strings."

"That's obvious, Sergeant. One of my men is pulled out of combat and put on fluff duty at the Pentagon. Doesn't take Sherlock Holmes to figure out someone's playing politics."

"This isn't what I want, sir. I requested EOD for a reason. I'm good at it, my squad is solid. My record stands."

"Then you had no part in this request for special treatment?"

"No, sir."

"Does General St. James know you're against this move?"

"Yes, sir." Max hesitated, torn between loyalty to his family and loyalty to his uniform. The uniform won. "My uncle sees my career as a stepping stone to bigger things. His feeling is that three generations of military service would look really good on a political bumper sticker."

Gilden winced. "Damn politicians."

"Exactly, sir."

"Be that as it may, your uncle outranks us both, Sergeant."

"This is clearly nepotism and backroom negotiating, sir. There has to be a way around it. Can't I lodge a formal complaint?"

"If it ever got through the red tape, it could get ugly."

Max stared at his feet. Even out of uniform, he wore boots. Solid, black, bulky. Made for defense. For standing on his own two feet. He'd be damned if he'd be railroaded.

What choice did he have, though? The Colonel was right. Lodging a complaint through official channels would get ugly. Lodging an argument over the dinner table was useless. Max knew from long experience that people in his family believed in the chain of command. They issued commands, others followed. In other words, the General didn't listen to anyone.

So...what? He was stuck?

"Can you talk to your uncle?"

Max shook his head. He'd already made himself clear. That his uncle had done this, despite Max's protest, indicated that he felt the discussion was over.

"My ETS is up in two months, sir," Max said swallowing the bile in his throat and taking a deep breath. ETS meant his term of service was finished. He'd signed on for another two years, but he'd be damned if he'd spend them playing toy soldier. "If I can't do my duty on the line, I'd prefer to step down. My papers guaranteed overseas service. If this reassignment isn't pulled, I'll file breach of contract."

Gilden rocked back in a creaky wooden chair and stared over steepled fingers.

"You'd walk instead of taking this transfer?"

Max hesitated. He'd never wanted to be anything other than a soldier. To serve his country. In Afghanistan, with his squad, he made a difference. Playing babysitter to a bunch of suits in uniform wasn't what he'd signed on for.

But serving was all he'd ever known. Ten years he'd been in the Army. He'd planned to retire a soldier, not to walk away defeated. But he'd choose defeat over dishonor. And taking a fluff job while his men, his friends, put their lives on the line was absolute dishonor.

"Yes, sir. I'd choose to walk."

WHILE SHE WAITED FOR GINA to bring back lunch, Sophia walked through the gallery. There was a couple in the smaller showroom, admiring the winery studies. The older man in the main showroom lounged on the settee, ostensibly looking at the black-and-white display of spring flowers. From the occasional snore, it was obviously afternoon nap time.

Unable to help herself, she slipped the camera from her pocket and snapped a picture. From behind, so his face was obscured, but his slouched position, chin on chest, made it clear he was cutting z's. "Art Soothes," she'd call it.

Smiling, Sophia was halfway through the next room before she realized she'd started naming her photos. As if someday, she'd actually put them in a show. She wasn't sure how she felt about ambition growing stronger than her fear of failure.

Maybe she had more confidence because Max liked her work. He'd insisted on seeing actual prints, claiming he couldn't tell diddly on the tiny view screen. So she'd printed a few of her favorites. Not any of the photos of him, of course. But one of the Golden Gate on a foggy morning, a couple of floral studies. Like her, his favorite had been the shot she'd taken of her family the morning before Rico had gone overseas. Using a timer, she'd squeezed into the shot at the last minute. Her father had been seated in his favorite recliner, with his sons ranging all around him and Sophia curled at his feet.

Max had been impressed with how strong each personality had come through in just a photo. Rico's wildness, Carlos' humor, Ben's thoughtfulness. Most of all, her father's pride.

Sophia was used to using her photos for clarity, to see to the heart of people or situations. She'd never thought that they'd provide that same gift to others.

So the idea of others seeing her work? Of deeming it worthy art? She wasn't quite there, yet.

But…maybe someday.

Which was safe, she assured herself. Someday was a nice, murky time way off in the future with no pressure.

Grinning at her own self-justification, she waved to Gina as the other woman came through the back with lunch, setting Sophia's on her desk for later.

"Go ahead and eat," she told her assistant. "I'll cover the front until you're done.

Twenty minutes and four additional pictures later, Sophia returned to her office. She was much less depressed now. So what if things weren't quite where she wanted them yet? And yes, Max was leaving but not tomorrow. They had a couple of weeks together. She was sure that a few more bouts of wild, hair-tangling sex and she'd be over this silly idea of falling in love.

She had to be. Her priority was the gallery. First, pulling it out of this mess, then working hard to make it the success she'd always dreamed of. After that, maybe she'd start thinking about other things.

Like letting that dream of being a photographer out of hiding. And falling in love.

Both equally terrifying.

Filled with a calm that she knew perfectly well was hiding the heartbreak underneath, Sophia unwrapped her salad, tore off a piece of tortilla and nibbled.

Then, fortified and ready to tackle the letter Gina had brought in earlier, she slit open the envelope and pulled out the papers. Yep, more legal crap.

She skimmed the cover letter. The tortilla fell from her numb fingers.

What the hell?

Horrified, she read the letter. The Historical Guild of Northern California was insisting that Esprit vacate the premises or they'd take legal action to sell the building. Since they, in effect, owned it and were only leasing it long-term—a

freaking century should count for something, shouldn't it?—
they were within their rights, the letter stated.

She had the phone in hand and had dialed Olivia before
she realized she'd moved. Ten minutes later, her shock had
faded into stunned horror.

"What do you mean, they have documentation? How can
someone document a lie?" she demanded.

"What they have is a case file of what the Historical Guild
feels is a breach of confidence," Olivia, who'd received her
own special delivery letter, replied. "Obviously whoever had
started those rumors about your sex addiction sent them doc-
umented evidence of what they see as the gallery's focus
on offensive fetishes. In the Guild's opinion the gallery isn't
supportive of their vision and policy."

"It all comes down to the gallery showing erotic art instead
of photographs?" Which had been going on for four freaking
years. So why now? Sophia ground her teeth together. Because
of Lynn, obviously.

"Yes."

"But I didn't do that. Joseph did. And we've stopped." Sophia rolled her eyes at her whiny tone. Way to stand up and
take control of her life. By sniveling like a three-year-old.

"What can I do?" she asked before Olivia could say anything. "How can I keep the gallery?"

In the long pause, Sophia could almost hear Olivia lining
up and discarding options.

Finally she sighed. "You're not going to like it."

"Just tell me," Sophia insisted with a sigh.

"Negotiate with Ms. Castillo. Split the estate so you can
access enough funds to purchase the building outright."

Automatic refusal was on the tip of Sophia's tongue. She
swallowed it back with an effort.

"I'll work up a list of suggestions," Olivia continued, obviously sensing Sophia's struggles. "I have notes on the specifics

your stepdaughter was especially adamant about. Perhaps we can find a middle ground. I'll get back to you in the next few days with suggestions."

Sophia made some sort of grunt that must have passed as agreement, because Olivia hung up. It took Sophia a while longer to unclench her fingers from the phone.

She hadn't lost the gallery.

She could buy it.

All she had to do was come up with a whole lot of money in the next ninety days.

"Does it all look okay?" Sophia asked Max the next afternoon as she set out a tray of cookies and a bowl of sugared nuts on the small sofa table in her office. She was expecting von Schilling any time now.

Max didn't know which made him hungrier—the sugar glistening off the chunky peanut butter cookies, or the sight of Sophia bending over, her black skirt stretched temptingly over her hips.

He knew which he wanted more. But he was pretty sure lusting after Sophia's body was fogging up his clear head. He knew damn well that she needed help. She was over her head and going down for the third time. There had to be some way he could save her from drowning.

"Who's trying to shut you down, again?" he asked, hoping he'd heard her wrong.

"The Historical Guild of Northern California," she said, barely paying him any notice as she busied herself with a silver tea service.

The name didn't help. California was full of do-gooder clubs and historical societies. His mother served on a million of them. He remembered his first night home and her talking about a problem her gang was having with some building or other.

Could she have meant Esprit? No. Of course not. She wouldn't do something so underhanded. Tabby would have the decency to confront the business owner and give her a chance to make things right. Wouldn't she?

His shoulder blades twinged from the recent stab wounds in his back he'd recently incurred from his uncle. Maybe that underhanded, as-long-as-I-get-my-way-I-don't-care-how-I-screw-you habit was contagious.

Hell, he was guilty of it himself. He thought of the money he'd handed over to the busboy across the street to watch the gallery building and the online snooping he'd done on Lynn Castillo. He'd even planned to drive up to Tahoe, where she lived, and confront her in person. But his career suddenly crumbling yesterday had got in the way of that scheme.

But the things he'd done, they'd been to help Sophia. He only had her best interest at heart.

"I wish you'd let me lend you the money so you can just buy the building," he offered again. He didn't even have to wait for her to shake her head to know what her response would be.

He didn't know if her independence was sweet or stubborn.

Probably both.

"That's kind of you, but no. I couldn't. I'll make this happen myself," Sophia insisted. She gave Max a determined smile and claimed, "One way or another, I'll work it out."

His jaw worked as he tried to keep from telling her that one way or another wasn't good enough. Even though she'd finally given in and decided to do a show with von Schilling, it was going to take more than one show to bring in enough money to buy the building.

Unable to do anything else, Max grabbed her hand and tugged so she tumbled into his arms. Soft meets hard.

Hand behind her neck, he pulled her down for a kiss. Her

lips were magic, sending a shaft of heat straight through his body. His tongue slipped between her teeth, tasting, teasing and tempting. His ego, among other things, soared when her body went lax, her breasts pressing tight against his chest.

Mmm. She was delicious. He wanted to lose himself in her arms. To let all the worries and decisions fade in the face of such hot temptation. He wanted to explore all the sexy possibilities she was offering.

She slowly pulled her lips away from his and gave his chest a pat, then levered herself to her feet.

She checked the coffeepot and the hot water for tea for the fourth time. "You don't have to stick around, you know. I can handle this meeting on my own."

"The guy's a perv," Max pointed out. "He takes pictures of naked women. Maybe I'd be jealous leaving him alone with you."

"Maybe you should be," Sophia teased.

"After all," she continued, "he's seen it all. Done it all. And recorded it all on film."

Max nodded, getting up to swipe a cookie off the tray. He wandered the room for a few minutes, then dropped to the couch again.

Picking up on his restless stress, Sophia stopped fussing around the office. She sat next to him and rubbed a comforting hand over his knee. "What's going on?"

"Nothing." At least, nothing he planned to talk about until he'd figured out his new career. And made sure Sophia wanted him around. He took a bite of the cookie. Mmm, good. Almost as tasty as Sophia herself.

"Are you sure?" She frowned, her blue eyes shining with concern. "I know I've been a little obsessed with my own problems today, but you really do seem off-kilter. Maybe later, we can get dinner and talk. If you don't have something else to do, of course."

He winced, the peanut butter cookie turning to dust in his mouth. He had absolutely nothing to do. At twenty-eight, his career about to go up in flames, his family was sure to disown him when they found out his plan, and he didn't know if the woman he loved wanted him to stick around past the end of the month.

A chilly terror moved through his body. He ignored it, as always, pushing emotion aside. A man didn't survive defusing bombs if he let emotions in. He'd deal with all of his problems later, after he'd fixed things for Sophia.

After all, ladies should always come first.

"Dinner sounds great," he finally told her. "I'm all yours, babe."

11

Sophia took a deep breath, not sure why the idea of Max being all hers made her stomach a knotted mess. Maybe because he looked so miserable about it?

Worried, she watched the impatience roll off him like an early morning San Francisco fog. She wanted to help. She really did. But she had enough experience with stubborn men to know he'd tell her when he wanted and not a second sooner.

Unless maybe she asked naked. Something to try later. Sophia gave a happy little sigh, knowing that image would get her through this afternoon.

Sophia tried not to chew her lipstick off, but, man, she was nervous. Von Schilling was her hero. The man was a photographic genius. And she was going to meet him. Meet him and discuss his show in her gallery.

She hurried to her desk to reapply her ruined lipstick.

"Mr. von Schilling," she said half an hour later. She forced herself to offer the plate of cookies to the man seated on the tapestry couch instead of throwing it at his head like she wanted. "I don't understand. Why did you contact me if you didn't want to do a show?"

"Hans, please," the gray-haired septuagenarian insisted.

"And what do I want with a show? Things like that, they belong in the material world. I'm old. I've disavowed the material world in search of a higher spiritual realm. I have no need for adulation and groveling."

"You have need of money, though," muttered the woman sitting next to him.

There were four people sitting in Sophia's office—herself and Hans, one of the most celebrated photographers of his decade, Max, who was silently watching from behind her desk, and Lily, von Schilling's daughter.

Lily was beige. Beige hair, beige skin, beige clothes. She sort of faded into the tapestry fabric of the couch. Her father, on the other hand, seemed to suck in all the light and color from the space around him. Long and lanky, he looked like the crooked man from that kid's poem. Knees and elbows poked out at odd angles, not softened at all by his loose hemp pants and shirt, both held together with drawstrings. He'd obviously never left his hippie days behind.

And then there she was, all prepared to graciously accept von Schilling's request to do a show, then flex her negotiating muscles by getting him to agree to a higher commission. Smart move when she'd thought he was desperate to show and she was his only option.

Now? Now she had a guy who didn't want to do a show she really didn't want to give. And now she had to talk him into it? Sophia gave Max a desperate look, but he just shrugged, his expression as baffled as hers.

"Why are you disavowing the material world?" she asked, more to buy time to figure out how to rescue this situation than because she cared.

"I no longer need physical constraints. I have closed the book on that phase of my life," he declared, his tone echoing eerily through the room. Like one of those TV psychics she remembered watching as a child at one in the morning when she'd snuck out of bed for a snack. "The constant focus on outside demands creates a ripple in my chi."

"Right," Lily said, finally speaking up. "But don't forget that Guru Wolfdragon said you can't move forward until all of the baggage of the past is released."

Wolfdragon? Sophia mouthed to Lily. The younger woman rolled her eyes and sighed, then in a subtle gesture out of Hans's line of sight, rubbed her thumb and forefinger together.

Ahhh, Wolfdragon must be from the Guru school of con artists.

"The photos are baggage?" Sophia guessed. And from the look on Lily's face, she was worrying a little that the baggage might end up a donation to the guru's retirement fund.

"They tie me to the past," Hans declared. "I no longer live there and am ready to move on."

"Okay, so you want to move on." Baffled, Sophia stared at the two of them. "But if you don't want to exhibit your photographs at Esprit, why has someone been calling weekly, nagging me to do a show?"

Sophia wanted so badly to rub her forehead and try to massage away the ache there. From what he'd said so far, Hans had spent most of the seventies stoned and never recovered. He'd walked away from his art, claiming the stress of photography was at odds with his Zen.

More likely, his daughter had cut off his dope supply and insisted he get clean.

"Hans is going to do this show," Lily broke in, her voice quiet, but firm. "His various…hobbies have sunk him in debt. His financial advisor suggested he sell off all those photos that are gathering dust in the attic. He won't sell direct to the public, though. He claims it's against his artist ethics."

"Plebeians." Hans dismissed her around a mouthful of cookie.

His daughter ignored him, continuing in her soft, almost

nothing voice. "This will be his final show. The goal is to sell his entire body of work. His contract with Esprit de l'Art requires that he show them here."

Sophia glanced over at Max, who was leaning back in her desk chair reading the contract. He met her eyes and nodded, then gave a slight head tilt toward the calendar hanging on the wall next to him.

A reminder, she knew, that the only way the show would be held at the gallery was if they did it next week before word got out that the building was being sold.

Sophia didn't bother freaking out. There wasn't time. If she did this show right, and von Schilling was serious about this being his final show, a huge thing since it would be his first in twenty years, then she stood to make enough for a solid down payment on the building.

Her gallery, and her future, lay in the hands of a man wearing embroidered silk bedroom slippers and beads in his goatee.

"I'll be happy to host the show," she heard herself say. "But we'll have to have it the weekend of the fourteenth."

"That soon? Isn't it a holiday?"

"That's the only weekend I have available," she claimed. "And I think tying the show in with the romance and glamour of Valentine's Day will be a wonderful promotional tool."

"SO WHAT'RE YOU DOING for Valentine's Day?" Gina asked as she uncrated yet another stunning framed black-and-white photo. This one of a topless cabaret dancer, one leg stretched to amazing lengths as she bent over a wooden spindle-back chair. "Hot plans for the most romantic holiday of the year?"

"I'm working on Valentine's, same as you," Sophia said.

Exhausted, she shoved the long swing of hair off her face and leaned back on her heels. It was casual night in the back of the gallery with she and Gina both in jeans. Gina's were shredded every which way, held together with band pins, while her own were pure stonewashed comfort.

After her meeting with the von Schillings two days before, she'd called in every favor, used every contact she had to push a promotional blitz like none other. She'd even recruited Max, giving him free rein to contact his country club cronies, his mother's ladies' club grand dames and any and all military personnel who might want to see some naked pictures.

Screw glamour and dignity. She'd pulled out Joseph's show playbook to use as a template. It'd worked plenty of times in the past, and even if she didn't like it, she knew it'd work now.

"A hugely successful gallery show, with promotion guaranteed from three newspapers, a magazine and a local TV crew," she muttered, unwrapping the paper from yet another half-naked dancer. "You know, ole Hans must've been tight with all the clubs here in the seventies. He's got cabaret, he's got ballet, he's got girls in go-go boots dancing in cages. And he got them all to take their tops off."

"Dude had a boob fetish," Gina agreed, her gaze skimming the twenty framed photos they'd already uncrated and leaned against the walls. "And quit changing the subject."

"I didn't. I told you my plans." Then, because her calves were killing her, Sophia gave up all semblance of dignity and dropped flat to sit on her butt. She tilted her head, squinting at the six-photo series of a go-go dancer, trying to figure out what it was about the images that were nagging at the back of her brain.

"You could be doing the romantic thing after the show," Gina pointed out. "I am. I'm having midnight drinks and dinner with Art of Defiance."

Sophia's gaze cut to the rock band pins keeping her assistant's jeans from unraveling. "Which member?"

"The whole band." Gina waited for Sophia to pick her jaw up off her chest before giggling. "I'm their greeter girl for the after-party. Handing out carnations, Hershey's kisses, that kind of thing. I might get lucky, though, and the guitarist will ask me out."

"That sounds...romantic?"

"No," Gina corrected with a happy shrug. "That sounds like sex. Which I hope you'll be getting, along with something really romantic for Valentine's. Hearts, flowers, chocolate. Bling is always good, too."

"All I'm getting is sex," Sophia assured Gina. Despite the fact that she and Max had spent almost every waking minute together the past week, she had no illusions that she'd be receiving red roses, nuts and chews or anything glittery. Unless, of course, any of those came with her goodbye hug. Max was scheduled to leave the Wednesday after the show. Heading back overseas where he'd face down bombs and bad guys.

Not a bad thing, given how important she knew serving the country was to him. But still, part of her wished it was a temporary goodbye instead of forever.

Blinking away the tears, she focused on rubbing a non-existent smudge off her jeans. Since when was an incredible sex life something to cry about? She had what she wanted. So what if she'd fallen in love with Max? Everything had a price. Apparently, the cost of the best sex of her life was a broken heart. It was worth it.

It had to be.

"The show will be romantic enough," she eventually said. She ignored the long, worried look Gina gave her and hurried on. "Don't you think it's clever to tie the holiday in by calling it Ode to Love? It's my attempt at de-eroticizing the displays."

"You don't really consider these erotic, do you?" a voice said from the doorway.

Gina giggled and offered Max a little finger wiggle, while Sophia just shrugged, leaning back against a crate and letting her eyes take in the man standing in front of her. He just kept looking better.

He still wouldn't tell her what was bothering him. He claimed it wasn't anything important. But he had a look in his eyes, half sad, half furious, that made her heart ache.

"I think I'm getting immune to erotic," she told him with a smile, hoping to cheer him up. "You've ruined my prudish side."

"Nah. I'm sure it'd resurface pretty fast if someone tried to plunk another four-foot dick in the middle of one of your shows."

"Only if it had Christmas lights wrapped around it," Sophia teased. Max's smile flashed. He reached down and took her hand, pulling her to her feet.

"We're going to take a break," he told Gina as he wrapped an arm around Sophia's shoulder.

"It won't be a long break," she told Gina, curving her own arm around Max's back. He was hard, warm and smelled wonderful next to her. Whenever she was this close, she just wanted to eat him up.

"My apartment?" she murmured quietly.

"Your office would be better," he decided, steering her down the hallway. Sophia frowned. The office meant no sex. At least, it usually meant no sex. There had been a couple of times…

"What's up?" she asked him when he closed the door and released her.

"How's the show coming along?" he asked.

Sophia narrowed her eyes. He had something else on his mind, but she was willing to play along. "We're doing pretty well. Von Schilling's got enough inventory for an entire show on his own, but we're pulling in a couple other photographers anyway to balance his with some less controversial displays."

"But you've got a pretty good handle on it all?" He stood

there, rocking back on his heels and looking as casual as ever. But she had the feeling he was mentally pacing.

"I think so," she said slowly. Not that she had a clue how to deal with her vandal. The creep had hit twice in as many days. Once spray-painting trash on the back door, then this morning calling the paper to put in an ad stating the cancellation of the show. Luckily Sophia had spent so much time on the phone with the editor of the lifestyle section that he'd called her to confirm before running it.

Had Max figured something out? Was that why he looked so serious and stressed? Or was it because he hadn't?

"Are you arranging for security so there isn't a repeat of the last show?" he asked.

"I…" The man knew her panty size and what flavor body oil she liked. He'd held her hand while she fell apart, listened to her dreams. And he knew damn well the state of her bank account. So why was she embarrassed to tell him she was too broke to afford security for the show?

"Will you let me take care of this for you?" he asked quietly. "I'll call in a few favors, get a few guys I know who're on leave to stand around and look tough. Low cost, no long-term commitment."

Sophia bit her lip. She needed this. She knew she did, and Max had made it as palatable as possible. There was a fine line between stubborn pride and idiocy. She might toe that line regularly, but she wasn't going to jump over it.

"I'd appreciate that," she told him, stepping closer so she could wrap her arms around him. His hands soothed a comforting path up and down her back and she let herself relax. Eyes closed, her ear against his heart, she listened to the steady beat.

What would she do without him?

"I've taken care of a few other things, too," he said, his voice a low rumble. "Some of mine. Some of yours."

Not sure why she suddenly felt like a scary cloud of gloom

had drifted into the room, Sophia slowly pulled back and looked into his face.

No smile in his eyes. The grim set of his jaw.

"This doesn't sound good." She stepped out of his arms and leaned against her desk. The look on his face made her think she was going to need the extra support.

"No, it's all good," he assured her. He shoved his hands in the front pockets of his jeans, the move emphasizing another good thing, which was how happy he'd been to have her in his arms.

Telling herself not to get distracted, Sophia crossed her arms over her chest, arched one brow and waited.

"First off, I received a change of orders," he told her. Sophia's breath caught in her throat as she noted the fury lurking in his dark eyes. "I was reassigned stateside."

Her heart leaped in joy. He wasn't leaving the country? She could still see him. Then she remembered the look on his face when his uncle had suggested a change in orders.

"I didn't think there was much call for EOD stateside," she said slowly.

"There isn't. If I'd taken the assignment, I'd have served at the Pentagon."

"If?" She actually heard the giddy bubbles of joy popping over her head.

"I refused."

"I didn't know you could do that."

"Under most circumstances, no," he acknowledged. "But I'd already termed out. My re-up contract specified EOD service in a battle zone."

She forced herself to only show calm interest, but her nerves were jumping like water on a burning skillet.

"I've notified legal that unless they correct this breach of contract, I'll be leaving the service." His words were emotionless. His face was expressionless.

And Sophia could clearly see he was miserable.

How could she be thrilled in the face of such horrible pain? But it wasn't as if she'd messed up his orders, right? She hadn't encouraged or pushed him to leave the service. Hell, she'd never once said a word about it.

She hadn't mentioned the terror felt by those left behind when someone they loved was in battle.

She'd even managed to keep herself from begging him to promise her a future, when she knew from Rico that pressure like that only made service more difficult.

So why did she feel guilty?

Maybe because while she hadn't done any of those things, she'd definitely thought about them.

"I'd think the Army would be more meticulous in their assignments," she said quietly, trying to figure out what was beneath the surface of his anger.

His stare was lethal. The anger wasn't directed at her, but in those few moments it occurred to Sophia that he knew her inside out. Max knew her dreams, her goals, her fears. He knew what she wanted and what stood in her way.

And she knew almost nothing about him.

Unable to stand it any longer, Sophia pushed way from the desk. She wanted to pace, but didn't think he needed the added stress.

"The Army isn't behind this problem," he admitted. "This is direct nepotistic interference."

It only took her about three seconds to figure that out. "No way. Your uncle?"

"Exactly."

Stunned, she dropped into the wingbacked chair and stared.

"Are you going to let him get away with this?"

"There is no getting involved. The chain of command is clear."

Sophia stared. Far be it from her to tell someone how to

get pissed off. But, holy cow, shouldn't he be doing something here?

She started to ask what his uncle had said, then stopped herself. She opened her mouth to ask what he'd do now if he wasn't going back to Afghanistan. Then she pressed her lips together. Her heart screamed at her to hurry up and nail down the details on their future together. Did they have one? How would this affect it? Them? Were they a them if they weren't temporary?

Her brain spun. Her stomach churned. Her nerves were shot, so she gave in to the need for comfort and pulled her knees up to her chest and wrapped her arms around her legs.

Why wasn't he saying anything else?

"You said you'd taken care of some things?" she murmured, needing a distraction to give her time to collect herself. "Was this the 'yours' part?"

"Yes," he said, nodding and shifting his stance.

"And the mine part would be?"

He paused, looking like he was gathering his thoughts, then shifting gears. He walked over to the desk and, in the same spot she'd stood a few minutes before, leaned against it and crossed one ankle over the other.

"The yours part is I've solved some of your gallery problems."

"You what?"

"I've had someone watching the gallery and we've—"

"Wait," she interrupted. "You've had someone watching my building?"

"Right," he said with a nod. "The culprit rides a motorcycle. I have a partial plate number and talked to the police."

Before he could say anything else, Sophia held up her hand. She shook her head, trying to clear the buzzing from her ears.

"You did what?"

"Look, the police have a lead now. We can talk about that later. The important thing here is that you want to keep the gallery and make it a success, your vision of success." He paused. She guessed he was waiting for her to agree, so she nodded.

"In order for the gallery to be that vision, you have to come up with the money to buy the gallery."

He paused again. This time she didn't humor him with a nod. Instead she stared, waiting.

"You need money. You need a great deal of money and luckily you have a direct line to it. I just cleared things out of the way so you can use that line to reel it in."

"You took out a loan?" she guessed with a frown. He'd better not have after she'd told him she wouldn't borrow money from him. But if he was staying, and they were a couple, maybe down the road they'd be more like partners. Him the silent partner with the money, of course, and her the vocal partner in charge.

"I hired an attorney," he corrected her. "He's the biggest shark in the Bay area and after reviewing your case, he's sure he can win it before the building is put up for sale."

"But Olivia is already negotiating a settlement," she said blankly.

"You shouldn't have to settle for half. It's all yours and you should fight for it."

Sophia saw black spots in front of her eyes. The room swam in a greasy wave of fury, making her ill it was so intense.

"Let me get this straight," she said quietly, trying to keep her tone even. "First you found a lead to who is behind the vandalism but didn't bother to tell me you were even looking. And then you went behind my back and hired an attorney? Filled him in on the details, the private details, of my situation? You paid his retainer out of your own pocket. A pocket that's now going to need to hold tight to its pennies since you're out of work."

"My career isn't the issue here," he told her, his words a little tight. As if he'd caught on to her anger and was feeling defensive. As well he should. She wanted to hit him over the head with something, so defensive was smart on his part.

"Your career isn't the issue? Why do you get to decide that?" she demanded. "You poke your fingers all through my career. What makes you so special that yours is off-limits?"

"Mine isn't in danger like yours is," he said, biting the words off as if they tasted nasty. Which, considering she could see the angry awareness in his dark eyes, she figured they must.

"Really?" She knew it wasn't fair to throw his destroyed career back in his face. She knew he was hurt and upset and feeling betrayed. But dammit, so was she.

Maybe if the *her* news hadn't come so close on the heels of the *his* news, she'd have been able to control herself. She'd had a whole three minutes of happiness and hope for a future together before he'd proven to her that there was no chance in hell they'd last beyond today.

She surged to her feet and started pacing.

"Because I could have sworn your career had just blown itself all to bits, Sergeant," she tossed over her shoulder. His wince didn't make her feel any better. If anything, being a bitch just made her feel angrier.

"How dare you," she snapped, the rope on her control fraying with each step. "Who the hell do you think you are?"

"I'm the man who cares about you and wants to make sure you get what you want, dammit."

"You?" she retorted. "You can't even stand up to your own uncle and save your own dream career. So what gives you the right to decide what's necessary to save mine?"

For a second she thought she'd gone too far. His entire body froze. His glare made her want to hide under her desk. She waited for him to yell. To throw something. Nerves jittering, she shifted away from the chair in case he decided that'd be the best missile to send flying across the room.

But Max did none of those things. His glare faded to ice. He pushed away from the desk, his eyes locked on hers.

Then, without another word, he walked out the door.

She wished he'd thrown the chair.

12

MAX STORMED INTO HIS mother's house, letting the heavy door slam behind him with a loud boom. Like a bomb detonating. How apt, he thought. After all, his entire life was exploding around him.

"Maximilian, what is wrong with you?" his mother demanded, halfway down the stairs, glaring at him like he'd just pulled a gun on her. Or spilled wine on her carpet.

"Did you know Uncle Charles pulled strings and had me assigned stateside?" he demanded.

From the look on her face and the infinitesimal shrug, it was clear his mother had known perfectly well what her brother-in-law had done.

"He had no right," Max said. "Neither did you. What the hell is with you people that you think you can sneak around behind people's backs and screw them over?"

"Watch your language, Maximilian."

"Or…what? You'll destroy my career?"

Shit. Max shoved his hand through his hair and ground his teeth. Son of a bitch. He hadn't meant to say anything about that. Confrontations were futile in his family. The men clammed up in stubborn silence and Tabby melted into a puddle of tears when the yelling started. In Max's experience, confrontations never led to resolutions. It was like trying to talk to the fanatic who just got a charge out of detonating a bomb.

Pointless.

"I can't believe you're taking that attitude after all we've done for you," Tabby said. Typically, her words were accompanied by a teary-eyed sniff. "Your career is our business. Your father and I had a plan. When he died, your uncle stepped in to ensure the completion of that plan."

She led the way into the parlor, stopping just short of swiping the back of her hand over her forehead to declare herself the queen of the martyrs.

"Dad might have wanted me to do things his way, but he understood when I didn't," Max said, standing in the doorway.

Well, that stopped the waterworks. Tabby turned, jutting out her chin. She hated talking about his father. Apparently this family was all about holding things in and manipulating behind one another's back.

"When he wanted me to go to West Point and I enlisted instead, he was angry but he understood. Then he wanted me in communications. I trained in EOD."

"He worried about you."

"But he understood."

Tabby's jaw worked, then she gave a slow nod. "He did. And he was proud of you."

"Then why can't you be proud, too? Why would you ruin what I've worked so hard for?"

His mother stared for a long, drawn-out moment. Then she shook her head. "It's for your own good, Maximilian. You are too close to the situation to be objective."

"Too close to my own life?" he asked incredulously. "You've got to be kidding."

"Your uncle has already made arrangements. There's no point arguing about it," she said quietly. Then, as if she was afraid of what he'd say next, she made a show of looking at her watch. "I have to run, Maximilian. I have a meeting with my, um, with a friend... An employee. With, well, a lunch thing. We'll discuss this later, shall we?"

And with that confusing announcement, that was that. Stunned, Max just stood there as she swept from the room.

He strode into the parlor and dropped onto the couch. Everything he was so pissed about—the manipulations, the arrogant decisions *for his own good,* the lack of respect toward his choices—he'd been doing the exact same thing to Sophia. Just like everyone else in her life had. And yet, she'd found a way around it.

Maybe once he'd made it up to her, she'd help him figure out how to fix this mess.

Two days later, Max strode through the doors of Esprit and stopped, stunned.

"Holy shit," he muttered.

It was incredible. Instead of a huge, empty—albeit elegantly empty—expanse of polished wood flooring, white walls and a few framed photographs lined up like soldiers in formation, the room was filled. Filled with color, with motion, with imagery. Framed photos still lined the walls, but at varying heights that drew the eye. Rather than a bare floor, there were easels strewn in what looked like a strategic pattern to move people through the room toward the back. Candles were lit in wall sconces he'd never noticed before, and sweet-scented flowers burst from round vases in wooden pillars. The red velvet settees were still there, but next to each was a small table. Probably to set drinks or food on, he imagined.

"What do ya think?"

He'd been so focused on the room he hadn't noticed Gina come in. Max turned. He stared. He blinked a couple of times, then shook his head. Even if he had noticed, he wouldn't have realized it was her until he'd heard her voice.

"I think it's very different," he said, his brain trying to take in what his eyes were seeing. Gina was…normal. Smooth black—and only black—hair, tucked neatly back in a lacy headband. Minimal makeup, wire-rimmed glasses and a simple black dress without a rip, tear or pin anywhere. Sure, she still had metal glinting off her face and her shoes looked like something Frankenstein might wear. But all in all, she looked normal.

He didn't understand.

"Why's everything so…"

"Uptight?" Gina offered when he hesitated.

Max grinned, not wanting to put his foot any further in hot water by agreeing.

The smile was enough for Gina, though. She went into her gameshow hostess routine, waving her arms and using a snooty tone. "The Ode to Love show will not only be featured on the evening news, there will be reporters of all sorts, reviewers and a guest list that reads like the who's who of Northern California. Rumor has it even the governor has been invited."

"Rumor?"

"Yep, a rumor started by me when I slipped his invite into that big blue mailbox up the street."

"Sophia really pulled out all the stops."

Gina looked around and nodded. "She said this is her last chance. It's the show she's always wanted to give, but was saving for the right artist."

"I guess right's subjective when you're on the edge of a cliff."

Gina wrinkled her nose. "Actually, this exhibit is amazing. If you get past the nipples, it's some of the best photography I've ever seen."

Max wanted to ask how much she'd actually seen to make that judgment, but he didn't want to have to deal with two pissed-off women tonight. Sophia herself was going to be difficult enough.

Then he looked at the pictures. Actually looked past the pomp and décor.

"Damn," he breathed. Gina was right. They were stunning. The play of light against shadow. The pictures all told a story, some subtle, some harsh. One photo in particular caught his attention. An elderly woman holding a toddler. The contrast of the woman's skin, wrinkled and spotted, against the pure unblemished sweetness of the little girl's was moving. But what really told the story were the eyes. The same shape, and even though the photo was black-and-white, Max was sure they were the same color. There was a touching continuity in the photo. A reminder that life circled.

"These are Tristan DeLaSandro's photos," Gina told him. "He's one of the artists Soph's been wanting to bring in. He's got some erotic stuff, too. It's in the back two rooms with von Schilling's work."

"Is von Schilling's this good?"

Gina nodded. Before she could say anything, they heard the rat-a-tat-tat of high heels from the hallway.

Sophia.

Max turned to face her. Gina scurried away.

Sophia stopped just inside the arched doorway, one hand on the wall as if to steady herself.

"What're you doing here?" she asked, her tone more breathless than confrontational. Good. He was tired of confrontations.

"I told you I'd handle security for this evening's event," he reminded her quietly. Did her eyes dim a little or was it just wishful thinking on his part?

The sight of Sophia in another of those sexy little black dresses made him want to drool. This one had wide straps that crossed over her shoulders and breasts, a glittery sort of belt that made her waist look tiny and a skirt short enough that he could get his hand up without her worrying about wrinkles. She'd paired it with a pair of sexy little black strappy sandals and black hose that had a seam up the back. He'd spent half his teenage years and all of his adult life fantasizing about stockings like that.

He wondered for a second if she'd known he was coming, and somehow tapped into his deepest sexual desire and worn them just to torture him. Given how angry she'd been when they'd last spoken, he wouldn't put it past her.

"What do you need to set up the security for the evening?" she asked calmly. He could see the hurt in her eyes. Knowing he'd put it there made him ill.

He'd make it up to her, though. Just as soon as this evening was finished.

"A couple of buddies will be here within the half hour. We'll mingle, guard and generally make sure nobody lets loose their pet skunk. You do your thing," he told her reassuringly. "We'll make sure everything's secure."

Sophia gave a cute little wrinkle of her nose, looking doubtful. "Can you do this without being obvious?"

Max gave her a long stare. "The guys will be in fatigues and wearing guns, but they promised not to wear camo face paint, so they should fit in fine."

Her lips twitched. Max's shoulders relaxed a little. At least she hadn't lost her sense of humor. "They'll be dressed in suits?"

"Just like me," he said with a raised brow. Her eyes skimmed his body, light and quick. As if she were afraid if her gaze lingered anywhere too long, he'd get all turned on and grab her.

She was smart that way.

"Fine. Coordinate with Gina," she said, turning on that sexy little high-heeled sandal and walking away.

Max rocked back on his heels and considered. She looked as delicious from the back as she did from the front.

But he needed to keep in mind that the back, just like the front, was off-limits.

When she reached the arch leading to the hallway, she shot a long, considering look over her shoulder. He had no idea what the look meant. He had no intention of finding out.

But damned if she didn't get him rock-hard with just the flick of those long eyelashes of hers.

SOPHIA MOVED THROUGH the gallery with a friendly smile, playing the ultimate hostess. Guests with food and drinks, check. Happy faces and the occasional laugh, check. A comment here, an observation there about the photos, double check. It was all going great.

Von Schilling hadn't been willing to come to the show. Apparently public events *harshed his mellow*. But the other three photographers featured were all in attendance, charming the patrons into buying their work and, in Tristan's case, into a few trysts in the hallway.

She should be ecstatic. It was going even better than she'd hoped. Instead, though, she felt like screaming. It was like being in a pinball game. She was ricocheting from room to room, always looking over her shoulder to make sure she stayed away from Max.

She could barely concentrate. Every time she saw him, she pictured him naked. Then, just as her body started to heat up she'd remember how he'd totally overstepped her boundaries and hired that attorney and anger would chill her right down. If this kept up, she was going to catch a cold from the constant body temperature changes.

"Excuse me?"

Sophia almost jumped out of her heels.

"Sorry. Didn't mean to startle you," the elderly man said. He had one of the show brochures in his hand and, she noticed with a tingle of excitement, had circled quite a few of the featured photos. "I'd like to make a purchase."

"Of course," she told him, almost purring as she looked at the list he handed her. "Right this way."

Ten minutes later, it was all Sophia could do not to dance across the polished floor while singing "Money." What a fabulous night.

And because she was feeling so good and wanted to keep this great feeling, she decided this was the perfect time to tell Max to take his platoon of canapé-munching security wannabes and head on down the road.

Shoulders back, chin up and determination in place, she scanned the room. There, at the far end by the arched doorway she caught sight of a dark-haired man. She didn't need to see through the crowd to be sure it was Max. The heat curling in her stomach assured her it was.

She'd taken two steps when something caught her eye.

Oh, God, not again.

A movement across the room caught her eye. Max. Frowning, he gave her a long stare. Then he scanned the room, immediately honing in on the skunk curled up under the red velvet settee. Pepé Le Pew all tuckered out and napping.

Nobody else seemed to see it, though.

How could they not? It was lying there snoring, for crying out loud. Maybe because it was black-and-white, like the pictures?

Sophia looked at Max again, her eyes pleading. She was so close. The show was going so well, halfway through the evening without a hitch. They'd sold a third of von Schilling's inventory already, along with a large number of the other artists' work. Her commission would soon be enough for a down payment on the building. Not that she'd figured out how she'd get an actual loan or anything.

One step at a time, she figured.

First the down payment. Then collateral. Then a loan.

Only now she'd shuffled *Get the skunk the hell out of here* to the top of her list.

Max had apparently gotten her silent message. He gave her a nod and jerked his chin toward the doorway. Sophia pressed her lips together, then nodded.

Stepping into the room, she raised her voice so the dozen people milling about the room could hear her. "Ladies, gentlemen, if you'd join me in the main gallery, we'll be…" What? A dozen pairs of eyes stared at her, asking the same question that was ricocheting through her mind. She caught sight of Tristan DeLaSandro. Sexy as hell, he lounged against the wall with the look of a man who wasn't worried about a thing.

"We'll be joining one of our guest artists, Tristan DeLaSandro, who will be happy to answer any questions about his work." She wondered why nobody seemed to hear the hysteria in her voice.

Tristan was inches away. Tall, dark and all bad-boy artist, he had a half smirk on his face. Sophia cringed, waiting to get blasted.

"Nice distraction from the skunk," he murmured before continuing into the larger gallery. A few seconds later, she heard the soft timbre of his voice, then laughter as he entertained the crowd.

Max waited until the room emptied before slowly, carefully approaching the skunk. Sophia's mouth went dry. Both nerves and desire worked through her system. She knew this was a serious situation. A skunk spraying would ruin the event—and the photographs. But, oh, baby, watching Max work was like watching a sexy ballet.

He probably looked like this when he defused a bomb. All intent and focused, like a cat stalking its prey. He stopped at one of the easels and slipped a flat cardboard box from behind the display. With quick, soundless moves, he folded it together, stepped silently toward the settee.

Sophia held her breath, both in anticipation and in self-defense. The skunk didn't move when he dropped the box over its head.

Her hands pressed tight against her mouth, she watched him slowly, carefully slide the box onto its side. He closed the flaps and gently lifted it.

Still no noise from the box. And, thankfully, no stink. Before Max could take another step, one of his friends brushed past Sophia and took the box. She and Max watched him hurry through the arch. Sophia wanted to follow him, to make sure it didn't spray in the back room and that, please, oh, please, he didn't let it out by the building.

But her knees were too shaky for her to even attempt to walk.

Instead, she gave Max a horrified look.

"I thought you were securing the building," she whispered.

"All the doors are covered," he told her. "The only way that skunk got in here is if some woman carried it in her purse."

She wanted to dismiss that as ridiculous, but she knew better. Who the hell carried a purse big enough for a skunk, though? And more important, who hated her enough to cart a stink bomb under her armpit into a public place?

"St. James."

Together, they turned. One of Max's friends gestured them to the back room. Heart sinking, Sophia forced her feet to move. Max pressed one hand on the small of her back and she almost whimpered and threw herself into his arms.

"What's ruined?" she asked when she reached the storeroom where the caterer and staff had gathered.

"Nothing," Becca assured her. "The food's fine, the wine's fine. Nobody's messed with it."

"Someone sure tried, though," the big blond friend of Max's said. His haircut said he was military. His huge shoulders said he was a force to be reckoned with. It was the grin on his face that Sophia couldn't read, though.

"What happened?" Max asked, curving his arm around Sophia's shoulder. She didn't know if the move had been deliberate or habit. She didn't care. She shifted closer, needing his warmth and strength.

"Someone got into the catering truck and loosened the parking brake," Becca said, her lips white and trembling. "It hit the lamppost, and while everyone ran out to check it, somebody dumped the trays of canapés and fruit on the floor."

"Man or woman?" Max asked.

"Woman," Becca and Blondie answered.

"Back up food?" Sophia asked.

"Across the street in the cantina's kitchen," Becca confirmed. "I've already sent someone to get it."

Before anyone could say anything else, Gina popped her head in. "Soph?"

"In a second," Sophia said impatiently.

"Um, now would be better."

She glanced at Gina, noted the red splotches on her assistant's pale cheeks and how huge her eyes looked behind her boring glasses.

"What happened?" she said, ducking out from beneath Max's arm and hurrying over. She followed Gina into the hall where they wouldn't be overheard. The heat warming her back assured her that Max had followed.

"Someone called a tow company. There are eight trucks out there trying to tow patrons' cars away. Apparently they were told the exact ones to take."

"The most expensive," Max guessed.

Gina nodded. "I convinced them to leave, but just as the last one pulled away, a different company's tow fleet showed up."

Max cursed. He moved toward the door but before he could take a second step, Sophia grabbed his jacket. She was afraid if he left her, the building would collapse or something.

"Can you send one of the other guys?" she asked quietly. He gave her a long look, then unclenched her fingers from his jacket and held her hand. "Gina, find Allen. He's on duty in the main gallery. Wearing a butt-ugly tie with fish on it. Have him deal with the tow trucks. I'll get someone else to cover the front room."

Gina nodded and hurried out. Sophia gave him a grateful look. Before she could throw herself into his arms, though, another harbinger of doom called out.

"St. James, Louie sent me to find you," a huge man said in a gruff voice.

Sophia gulped. Like Max and the rest of the security team, he was dressed in a suit and tie. But unlike Max, who looked sexy and urbane, or the blonde, who looked like a buffed surfer going to church, this guy looked like The Hulk on his way to court. He had no neck, so the tie looked like it was hanging from his chin.

"What's up?" Max asked. She could feel the tension radiating off him, but his words were calm. She glanced at him. His face was calm, too.

She felt some of the tension draining from her own body.

"Someone tried to start a fire," The Hulk said.

The tension came back with a vengeance and brought a whole slew of terror with it.

"It's out. Some woman lit a trash can back in the office. Louie doused it with a pitcher of ice water before it caught hold."

"Oh, God." Sophia twisted her hands together. Her mouth went dry and spitless.

"Did he see who did it?"

"Yeah," the guy told Max. "He walked in on her. While he was watering she tried to run."

"And?"

"He grabbed her. Dumped another pitcher over her head when she kicked him. He's holding off calling the cops until you decide what to do with her."

"Where is she?" Max and Sophia asked together.

"Locked in the office bathroom."

"Take care of things," Max ordered.

Sophia didn't bother to protest his taking over. She was so grateful to have him here, she'd have curled up on the floor and cried if he hadn't taken charge.

Needing his strength, she slipped her hand into his and hurried along the hallway one step behind him.

"I thought I had it all handled," she said quietly, her words almost a whisper. "I did everything I could think of to make the show a success."

"And it is a success," Max pointed out. "We're just making sure it stays that way."

As they passed through the arches toward the hall that led to her office and the bathrooms, Sophia shot a quick glance at the showrooms. A few dozen people were milling through, talking, sipping champagne and enjoying the show. She saw Gina, clipboard in hand. Taking orders, Sophia knew.

A skunk, an attempted catering catastrophe and a fire. And they were still buying.

She'd celebrate later. After she'd thrown up.

They went into her office and stepped over to the closed bathroom door someone was pounding on. Max accepted the key from the guy standing guard. He gave a nod and the guy left, closing the door behind him. She could see his shadow against the etched glass of the door as he stood, arms crossed and his back to them. Ensuring privacy, Sophia realized.

Privacy was good.

"Ready?" Max said, holding up the key.

13

"WHAT IF IT'S LYNN?" Sophia winced. She hadn't meant to say that aloud. She knew the woman hated her. But to have to see proof, face-to-face, made her a little ill.

"Then we have her arrested."

Dread moved through her stomach like greasy smoke. She took a deep breath, trying to banish the sick feeling.

The pounding on the bathroom door continued.

They kept right on ignoring it.

Overwhelmed, Sophia closed her eyes and dropped her forehead against Max's chest. His arms encircled her, pulling her tight against him. She felt safe. Safe and loved. Breathing in his warm male scent, she realized that half of loving someone was trusting them. She'd been so afraid of giving up control, she'd refused to see the obvious. That Max was a man she could trust. With her life, with her business, with her heart.

"I need you," she finally admitted, lifting her head to meet his eyes. "I know I can deal with this. That's the important thing, right? That I can handle it on my own. That doesn't mean I have to be all stubborn and independent, though. I want you there…just for support."

Sophia waited for the roof to cave in. For Max to crow

in triumph or give her a condescending smile, as if he'd just been waiting for permission to run her life.

She got neither. Instead, he gave her a tight hug and whispered against her hair, "Sweetie, I'm here for you. Just for support."

She smiled against his chest, warmth and contentment like she'd never felt before centering her. Maybe, so busy trying to prove she could do it all by herself, she'd blown chances to let people show her that they believed in her.

Then she thought back to Joseph's passive-aggressive attacks and her brothers all-out bullying bossiness.

Nope. Max was just special.

"Ready?" he asked after a few seconds.

Sophia took a deep breath and stepped out of the safe haven of his arms. Whoever was on the other side of the door had added kicking to their pounding. Sophia winced. She'd rather stay wrapped around Max permanently, but she knew she had to face this head-on.

"Ready," she told him.

Max inserted the key into the shaking door.

He motioned her back, just in case Lynn came out swinging, she figured.

And he turned the knob.

The door swung open.

Sophia gasped. Her knees turned to jelly and her jaw hit her chest.

"What the…" Max growled.

"Oh, my God," Sophia breathed, dropping onto her tapestry couch when her knees gave away. "This is some kind of a joke, right?"

"Mom?" Max said, stunned.

FIVE MINUTES LATER, SOPHIA paced her office, tugging at her hair just in case it relieved a little of the pressure on her brain. "But… I don't understand."

"What's to understand? Insanity is beyond comprehension," Max muttered through clenched teeth.

Finally unable to deny the truth, Sophia threw her hands in the air and exclaimed, "Your mother is a vandal? The dame of Nob Hill? Mrs. General St. James, the committee queen?"

"I'm going to have to have her locked up," Max said, pacing opposite her and muttering. "Psychiatric evaluations. Therapy. House arrest. The press. Oh, hell, the press. This is going to be a nightmare."

"Going to be a nightmare?" Sophia exclaimed. "It's been a nightmare for the past two months. I can't believe this. She can't be responsible. Not all along. Can she? I didn't even know she was at the gallery tonight, for crying out loud."

Max shook his head, holding his palms up in a who-the-hell-knows move. Then he twirled his finger around his ear in the classic cuckoo sign.

"I'm standing right here, you know," Tabby stated in a snippy tone. She gave them both an icy glare. Her arms were wrapped around her chest like a straight jacket. Apt, Sophia figured, since she was apparently crazy.

"Since you're sitting here," Max growled, "how about you tell us what the hell is going on."

"I won't be talked to in that manner, Maximilian." His mother gave him a chilly look and lifted her chin. Faint color warmed cheeks still damp from the ice water deluge.

Class, Sophia realized. This was class. The woman's perfect hair was dripping down her back, she had tiny chunks of ice cube melting on her shoulder and she'd been caught trying to set fire to Sophia's bathroom. And she still looked as if she'd have a servant beheaded if the cold cucumber sandwiches weren't cut into perfect circles.

"What's going on, Mother?"

Apparently that manner of speaking was more acceptable to Mrs. St. James. She nodded and, after a brief glance at her options, sat in one of the leather wingbacked chairs. Sophia wondered if that was a courtesy so her wet self didn't ruin the upholstery, or if it was because nothing else was deemed worthy.

"The fire, the food, the vandalism. Was that all you?" Sophia asked Tabby, her head still reeling in shock.

"I had to stop the show," Tabby explained, looking at Sophia instead of her son. "I couldn't let…"

Sophia frowned. Couldn't let what? Before she could push, Max butted in.

"A skunk, Mother? Where the hell did you get a skunk? How did you get it in here? Twice?"

"SANALT."

"Huh?"

"What?" Max asked at the same time.

"Stinky Animals Need A lot of Love, Too. It's one of the groups the Ladies Club supports. I just drop by their shelter and check out one of the destunk skunks. The skunk's name is Andrew."

"That stinky little thing is named Andrew?"

"They don't spray, so they barely stink." Tabby gave Sophia a horrified look. "You don't think I'd risk carrying a fully loaded one, do you? No, these are more like kitty cats. They're litter-box trained, sweet and cuddly. Very good pets, actually."

"Pets?" Sophia repeated faintly.

"You use someone's pets as a threat," Max said, his voice strong and sure. Strong and sure enough to make both women wince. "You trashed Sophia's place, ruined her show and are now hauling skunks in your purse?"

"Oh, Maximilian, calm down. Of course I didn't do all of that." Tabby waved her perfectly manicured hand and confessed, "Bobby, the gardener's assistant, did most of the dirty work for me. Which is why my roses look so poor this year, to be honest. He's been so busy with this little side job."

Sophia shook her heard, trying to get rid of the buzzing in her ears. Roses? Really?

It was like being dropped into bizzaro land.

Next thing she knew, Tabby would break out in song and dance on the coffee table. It wouldn't surprise her one bit, either.

Dance.

Sophia caught her breath. No way.

She lifted her head and squinted at Tabby. Was it possible?

"Wait a minute," Sophia said slowly. Max gave her a questioning look but she wasn't paying any attention to him. She tried to pretend she was looking through a camera's viewfinder. Snap, she imagined.

Yep, and there it was.

"I know what's going on," she breathed, shock rocking through her system.

Max's mother narrowed her eyes, one disdainful brow arched as if she were calling Sophia a liar. Then she looked closer. She blanched, her face the same gray as the muted black-and-white photo behind her head.

"No, you don't," she dismissed. But her voice was shaky and she looked scared.

"What's the deal?" Max asked, directing his question to Sophia.

She gave him a long, considering look. "Maybe this would be easier if you waited in the hall."

Tabby nodded.

Max clamped his arms over his chest and stared.

Sigh. Sophia knew she shouldn't feel sorry for the woman who'd gone out of her way to cause so many problems. But now that she understood why. Kinda.

"You're the cage girl, aren't you?" she asked quietly.

Tabby burst into tears. Not ladylike and contained tears. Big, gulping sobs. As if the shell she'd carefully crafted had cracked and suddenly everything was gushing out. If she'd shown as much of her stuff as Tabby had in those pictures, Sophia figured she'd crack, too.

She grabbed a box of tissues and pressed it into the older woman's hand. Then, already wincing, she looked at Max.

He looked like a bomb had just exploded in his face.

MAX STARED, HORRIFIED. What should he do? Panic gripped his stomach. He stood, sat, then stood again. Should he go to her? Get a doctor? Run?

He liked the idea of running.

"What the hell is a cage girl?" he heard himself ask. Whatever it was, he was sure he'd regret finding out.

His mother cried harder. He winced, sinking down in the chair and wishing someone would throw an explosive into the room. At least he'd have something less dangerous that he'd know how to handle.

Sophia sighed, then apparently unable to watch the drama any longer, got up and moved over to sit next to his mother. She wrapped an arm around Tabby's shoulder and the older woman sank into her chest, bawling as if someone had told her she was broke.

"Sergeant?"

Max glanced at the door.

"Just wanted to let you know everything's under control out here. Louie said the skunk is in the back room drinking milk. The food and drinks are being served again. No sign of an accomplice. Do you want the cops called?"

Hell, no, he didn't want to call the police on his mother. The words were on the tip of his tongue, but he stopped. He slanted a look at Sophia. Her pale eyes stared back. Waiting.

"Ask Ms. Castillo," he said. "It's her call whether we call the police or not."

Tabby howled louder.

Sophia glared.

"What?" he asked. "I thought you didn't want me interfering in your life or poking my nose in your business."

"Don't be mean," she said, now giving his mother's back a soothing pat. "No, of course we won't need the police."

She stopped and bit her lip. Max could see the battle between wisdom and compassion going on behind that pretty face. Finally she said, "Unless someone else is involved. If there are any more threats or problems, I want the cops and my lawyer called."

Tabby shook her head, leaving a black smear on Sophia's shoulder. Max winced.

"No, no," his mother said in a small voice. "No threats. Nothing else."

Max waited for Louie to close the door behind him, then he dropped his head into his hands.

Sophia was right. Who was he to tell her how to fix her problems? He was the root of all of her problems.

"I don't understand what's going on," he said, finally raising his head to stare at the two women who'd apparently bonded. His mother and his girlfriend. All cozied up, buddy-buddy and giving him fish-eyed stares as if he was the bad guy here.

"Von Schilling's show includes a few photos of your mother," Sophia said.

Max frowned. "No, it doesn't. Those are all…"

Horrified, he broke off and stared.

First at Sophia.

Then at his mother.

Then at a spot on the wall behind them both where he hoped the blank space would cover the images in his brain.

"Oh, God." Max closed his eyes. The images wouldn't fade. He didn't know which one of those photographs had been of his mother. He didn't want to know.

His eyes popped open.

"This is the project you mentioned? The business you

thought was too controversial? You sicced the Historical Guild on Sophia?" he accused.

"What?" Sophia exclaimed. "Your mother's behind that?"

She pulled back to glare at Tabby. Then she and Max both grimaced at the sight of his mother's face, all swollen and blotchy. Mascara ran in streaks to her chin and her lips were white as she pressed them together to try to hold back sobs.

Sophia sighed, then pulled her arms tight again. Max's heart did a little flip-flop.

"You should have told me," she hissed.

"Why are you holding her so tight?" he countered.

She tried to glare, but he could see there was no heat behind it. Then she rolled her eyes and pulled back so Tabby had to look at her.

"You're going to convince the Historical Guild not to sell this building," she told his mother. "You owe me that."

Tabby nodded without hesitation.

"In exchange, I'll pull your photos from the display."

Tabby started bawling again.

Max just stared, baffled. He'd been prepared to bring in an attorney. To fight his own mother to protect Sophia's interests. And just like that, she'd taken care of it all by herself.

Max knew he should be glad. Thrilled and proud. But all he felt was a defeated sense of uselessness. Sophia had solved her problems with the gallery vandal. His mother had solved her apparent problems of her, oh, God, nudie shots. And him? He'd started out without any and now his entire life was a problem.

Needing air, he murmured something about letting the women figure things out together. He barely noticed Sophia wave him out of the room as he left.

MAX DIDN'T KNOW HOW HE found himself on the cement stoop in front of the plain one-story military house. He had no clue what he was doing here. It was pointless.

But while he'd always worked his way around confrontations, he'd never backed down from anything. Or anyone.

He glanced at the small brass plate next to the doorbell. General C. St. James. The lights were on, so he knew his uncle was home. That wasn't why he was hesitating.

Suicide missions done in the name of useless heroics had always pissed him off. And yet, here he was.

Ordering himself to get it over with, he rapped on the door. It took his uncle a minute to open it, then, after a frown, the older man silently stood aside to welcome Max into the house.

"Well, this is a surprise. What can I do for you?" the General asked after they were both seated in the den.

Max had to give the old guy credit. He was a strategist right down to his toenails. After his silent welcome, he'd bypassed the comfy living room with its welcoming fire and led the way down the hall, seated himself in the position of command behind his desk and waved Max into the leather seat opposite him.

"I'd like you to rescind the Personal Change of Status," Max said, getting right to the point.

"Request denied."

Exactly what he'd expected. Max raised one eyebrow and rested his hands on the studded arms of the chair. Nothing showed on his face. He'd just been schooled by the two most important women in his life about what it really meant to fight for something, and he'd be damned if he'd fail.

"I won't serve at some cushy job while we're at war," Max calmly stated. "Not while men are overseas risking their lives."

For a brief second, he saw a glimpse of pride in his uncle's eyes. But then he blinked and the stoic command was back in place.

"You have no choice," the General corrected. "Orders have been issued. You'll follow them."

"I do have a choice. And if these orders were for the good of anything other than your own personal agenda, I would follow them. But they don't benefit me, they don't benefit my unit and they don't benefit my country."

"Are you questioning my authority?"

"As my superior, no," Max said, knowing he was walking a very fine line. The road to family loyalty only went one way with his uncle. "But as your nephew, I'm saying you've crossed the line."

The General stared, his face blank. For a second, Max hoped he'd gotten through. Maybe the old guy would finally accept that Max was a good soldier, a credit to his uniform and, dammit, an adult who could make his own career choices.

Then the General shook his head. "The order stands."

Max's gut tightened. But he didn't hesitate before replying. "I'll ETS and leave the service."

"Bullshit."

"I've already informed Colonel Gilden that I was leaving."

"You signed reenlistment papers."

"I signed a contract that specified that I'd serve overseas in EOD. Unless you rescind this PCS, the Army is in breach of contract. I might have to serve the last month of my duty in Washington, but then I walk away. Honorable discharge."

His eyes locked with his uncle's. Neither man blinked, neither looked away. And Max knew that was it. He was out of the Army.

SOPHIA WAVED AWAY THE last of the cleaning crew and said good-night to Gina. Then, with a deep sigh, she locked the front door. She left the back unlocked, though. Max had to come back eventually, right? She thought of the roses and chocolates in her office and smiled. She had an early Valentine's celebration planned when he did.

She was equal parts exhausted and exhilarated. Since the two emotions didn't mix well, she felt a little woozy. The night had been seriously overwhelming.

But it was Valentine's weekend. And despite the weirdness of it all, her problems were solved. Well, mostly solved.

Before she could consider the ones that were left, Max walked through the back hallway. Joy filled her as she hurried forward to wrap her arms around his waist. She settled her face against his chest and gave a deep sigh.

"There you are," she murmured.

"You shouldn't be so quick to hug me," he said, stepping back just a little.

"Why? Did you bring Andrew the skunk back with you?" she teased. Then she got a good look at his face. He looked... stressed. "What's up? Where did you go?"

"I...had some things to deal with."

Sophia waited.

Max grimaced. "I just came back to apologize. I can't believe I didn't realize it was my mother. I tracked down the motorcycle. It belongs to one of the gardeners."

He paused. As if he were waiting for her to blow up at him or something. Sophia frowned and shrugged. "Apparently he moonlights."

"Be serious, Sophia. It was right there under my nose the whole time, and I didn't catch on. I almost let your big night be ruined."

"No way—" she started to say. But Max, apparently juiced up on guilt, interrupted her.

"I'm responsible," he said, his chin jutting out.

She was still puzzled, but now Sophia was getting pissed, too. Why was he ruining their cuddlefest?

"You've got to be kidding," she said incredulously. "How do you figure this is all about you?"

"I'm the one who pushed you to do the show with von Schilling," he said coldly. His tone was worthy of that big high society house he'd grown up in. Rigid, uptight and distant. "I'm the one who was supposed to provide security for the show and make sure nothing happened. And it was my mother who not only almost ruined your show, but who has spent the past month vandalizing your gallery, tried to evict you and destroy your business."

Sophia sucked in a deep breath.

"So let me get this straight," she said. "You're taking credit for the state of my career?"

The icy mask cracked. Brows furrowed, he gave a little shake of his head. "No. I'm taking the blame for its destruction."

"But I'm the one who made the choices I did. Your mother made her choices. Why can't *we* have the blame?"

"Because I should have stopped it, of course."

"Oh, fine. You win. You're so freaking bright, the universe should revolve around you instead of the sun. There's just no reasoning with you." Sophia threw her hands in the air. "It's all your responsibility. Obviously you don't believe I'm capable of running my own life when you can do it so much better for me. Which of my many problems will you solve next?"

He just stared at her. His soldier face. Blank, stoic, detached.

"There's only one that I see. And I've already solved it," he said. His words were even, his tone soft and quiet.

"You solved it, did you?" she asked, just as quietly. Hers wasn't a soothing tone, though. Nope, she just sounded bitchy. Sophia wanted to cry. She didn't want to sound bitchy. She wanted to sound romantic, sweet. To curl up in his lap and tell him how glad she was the problems were over, to give him big sloppy kisses, then start planning the rest of their lives—or at least their next few months—together.

"I did solve it, yes." The corner of his mouth twitched with the hint of a humorless smile and he shrugged.

"Care to fill me in?"

"I talked to my uncle. I told him how I felt. I made it clear that if he didn't step out of my career, I'd be leaving the service."

"You confronted him?" She should be glad, shouldn't she? He'd stood up for his career. For something he loved. And he was thanking her for pushing him to do it.

But she didn't feel glad. She felt scared.

"I met with him. We settled things. He'll stay out of my career from now on."

"What are you saying?" she asked. She knew. She'd known from the beginning but she'd let herself hope. She'd let her heart dream out loud that secret little hope she hadn't even admitted to herself when she'd pretended to be happy he'd be leaving at the end of the month.

Then, when he'd told her he was staying, she'd actually believed it could work. She'd have made him happy enough if he'd stayed. But how selfish was it to expect someone you loved to settle for enough?

"My original orders were reissued. I'm going back to Afghanistan. I leave Wednesday."

Sophia licked her lips, trying to find the words. Any words. Her mine was blank, engulfed in pain.

"I'll come see you before I leave," he murmured, reaching out to slide his hand through the heavy fall of her hair.

"No," she whispered, blinking fast. She wasn't going to fall into a puddle of mush and make him feel guilty. She wasn't going to mess with his head or try to make him second-guess his decision. "I'm going to be busy this next week. Despite the problems, the show was a huge success. We've got a series of smaller events all week. I'll be tied up here and need to focus. On business. On negotiating with your mother."

On learning to survive without him.

"This doesn't have to be goodbye," he said, even though his tone said he knew it was. "If you'd like, we can—"

"No," she exclaimed before he could finish the suggestion. She took a deep breath, then shook her head.

"No," she repeated, more calmly. "You know the rules. No baggage when you return to duty. Rico told me about that." He winced, but she shook her head. She didn't want him to feel bad. That was its own form of baggage and she'd be damned if she'd send him back to war lugging it with him.

"Max, it's fine. You're doing what you're meant to. And we knew we only had a short time. We made the most of it. It was a wonderful month, but now it's over."

Just like she'd intended. Wow, look at that. She'd made a plan, seen it through and got exactly what she'd said she wanted. And now he needed to leave before she started crying.

"Be safe," she said quietly.

She stood on tiptoe, brushing a soft kiss over his lips. His hands clenched her shoulders. Max gave her a long look. She could see the arguments in his eyes. Which meant he could probably see the pain in hers.

Then, finally, he nodded.

And he turned to leave.

She waited until the door closed behind him.

Just in case, she waited a few seconds more.

See. She was in complete control.

And then, unable to stand any longer, she threw herself on the couch and gave in to the tears.

14

THE NEXT MORNING, SOPHIA had cleaned the gallery and was now tallying sales. She had to keep re-adding, though, because the number on the calculator seemed too big to be real.

"I'm surprised you didn't use these photographs in the negotiations," Tabby said. She stood next to Sophia in the storeroom, wrapping the half-dozen framed photos of her wild cage times in innocuous brown paper. "If you pushed hard enough, I'd have probably bought you the building to keep these out of sight."

"Isn't it bad for negotiations to give that kind of information away?" Sophia asked, shoving aside the adding machine—was that number really right?—to help wrap one of the framed photos.

"Oh, no. We already made the deal and you won't go back on your agreement."

Sophia considered that and sighed. Yeah, Tabby was right.

"It worked out okay," she said with a shrug. "I got what I wanted."

Sort of. Now that the looming threat of being evicted was off her shoulders, Sophia didn't really know what she wanted.

Success, of course. But in what way? In the normal way— return the gallery to the old format and keep the boobs out of it? Or in the holy crap way—she'd made a lot of money last night and those photos really weren't porn?

"Why'd you do these photos?" Sophia asked, the words out of her mouth before she could stop them. Then, because she'd already put her foot in it, she continued, "I mean, I understand why you wanted to get them back. But why'd you pose in the first place?"

Tabby paused. She looked across the table with dark, intense eyes she'd passed on to her son and considered. She was back to society matron today. Her hair perfectly coiffed, her clothes dry and sedate. But there was a wicked light in her eyes that Sophia kind of liked. It made her more real.

"I guess I thought it was a good idea at the time," Tabby finally said. "I'd had a pretty sheltered upbringing and was free for the first time. Out on my own, independent, determined to make my mark."

They both glanced at the triple-matted photo framed in dark walnut. Her hair had been a waterfall, hanging straight and heavy to her hips. Thigh-high white patent leather boots, a barely-cover-the-essentials skirt whose fringe screamed shimmy. Peeking through all that hair was a perky rack like only a twenty-year-old could claim.

"And this was your mark?"

"It was one of them." Tabby gave a little smile and folded the paper, hiding her mark. "But then I met Marshall and realized that he wouldn't be comfortable with that. I had a choice. Continue with my little rebellion, or return to the life I'd grown up in, create a future and make my mark in other ways."

"So you gave up your dreams to get your man?" Sophia surmised.

"Goodness, you're making this into a much bigger deal than it actually was."

This from a woman who'd smuggled a skunk in her purse.

"I've made a point not to interfere in my son's life. He's got enough of that from his father's side of the family, after all. But I'm going to make a tiny exception right now and suggest that you and Maximilian sit down and talk to each other. I'm sure whatever the problem is, you can solve it if you want to."

"I doubt it," Sophia muttered. She'd let Max go for his own good. So she wouldn't—couldn't—do anything to solve the misery engulfing her.

"I know why he's so stubborn," Tabby said, folding the brown construction paper neatly over another framed photo. "But why are you?"

Emotionally numb, Sophia just stared.

"Maximilian was raised with expectations. He was told from the time he started walking what his life was going to be. My husband had huge plans for his son." Tabby paused her wrapping, lost in memories for a moment. Then she shrugged. "Some people would have rebelled and walked away from having their entire life outlined for them before they were out of diapers. Luckily, Max loved the Army. He'd never wanted to be anything but a soldier."

"So he fell right in line with what his daddy wanted."

"Oh, no," Tabby protested, holding out a length of twine and eyeing it before wrapping it around the wrapped frame. "Max was a smart one. He got what he wanted on his terms, not his father's. He's always been determined to go his own way. I expect that's one of the things he found so attractive about you. That independence."

Not attractive enough to want to continue a relationship with her, though. Sophia tried to stop her lower lip from trembling. She'd promised herself she was through crying, dammit.

"I didn't mean to upset you," Tabby said, sounding sincere

despite the stiffness of her words. "To be honest, while at first I thought the relationship might be serious, now I realize it's anything but."

Sophia heard the condemnation in those snooty words.

"How can we have a relationship thousands of miles apart?" Sophia asked, wiping at the tears streaming down her cheeks.

"It's doable, as I well know." Tabby arched a brow and gave Sophia a piercing look. "Of course, it doesn't matter since you're perfectly willing to let him go? You had all the means right there at your fingertips to make him stay but you refused to use them."

"You mean emotionally blackmail him into giving up his career?" Sophia glared. Did the woman never learn? Hadn't last night showed her that manipulation and sneaking around never paid?

"Don't be silly. You wouldn't ask him to give up his career any more than he'd ask you. That's not love, after all." Tabby added her last package to the stack on the hand truck and then gave Sophia a stern, penetrating look at odds with her fluffy society looks. "Or, well, I guess it's not love, anyway, is it? At least not on your part."

Shock was the only thing that kept Sophia from protesting.

Tabby shifted the hand truck into travel mode. "To quote my daddy, 'Until you step up to the plate and swing, you're just pretending to play the game.' In other words, you obviously didn't care as much as you claim, now, did you?"

Stunned, Sophia let her go.

Apparently it was time to put away the martyr wear and go get her man.

Before she could, the phone rang. She glanced at the caller ID. "Hi, Olivia. What's the news?"

"THIS IS NICE."

Sophia turned from her contemplation of the ocean and gave a shaky smile. She loved the estate, especially the gardens and this view. She was so glad to be able to share them with Max.

"I didn't think you'd come."

"You asked me to, so here I am," he said as he stepped farther into the garden. Her breath caught at the sight of him.

He was in uniform. God, he was gorgeous. He was always sexy, no matter what he was or wasn't wearing. But seeing him in uniform almost gave her a heart attack. Desire curled deep in her belly. Her nipples tightened and heat pooled between her legs. She wanted to check her chin for drool.

"I love this spot," she said, stalling. She had so much to say, so much on the line. And she was terrified. "It always makes me think of romance."

"Is that why you called me? You wanted a romantic goodbye?" He sounded both shocked and a little angry. She couldn't blame him, considering how she'd blown off his suggestion that they try to keep their relationship alive long distance.

"No. I didn't want to leave things ugly between us. What we have is too special for me to let you leave without telling you…" She couldn't do it. The words choked in her throat. Black spots danced in front of her eyes. She gulped and sidestepped. "Without telling you what I've done."

"What did you do?" he asked, a little half smile playing on his lips.

"I made a deal with your mother, the photographs of her in return for the Historical Guild not selling the building. And she's going to help me with some promotion for the gallery. The exhibit was such a success, I realize it'd be stupid not to show nudes. Tasteful ones, at least. And apparently, the nude photos only pose a problem for your mother if she's in them," she told him. His wince made her smile.

When he didn't say anything, though, she kept babbling. "I heard from my attorney yesterday, too. Lynn's agreed to settle. The battle over Joseph's will is over."

She tried to remember that incredible feeling of triumph

when Olivia had called to tell her they'd waved the white flag. But she couldn't get past the frayed knots of nerves in her belly.

Then Max's grin flashed, instantly relaxing her. Sophia automatically smiled back.

"Did you get everything?" he asked.

Sophia wrinkled her nose. "I got everything I really wanted. This estate, my jewelry, the cash holdings. She gets the business and stocks."

"That's great." He reached out and wrapped one arm around her shoulder, pulling Sophia close and giving her a quick kiss.

"Congratulations. Your life is exactly what you wanted now," he told her. "You've settled the will. Your gallery is both successful and safe. And you've reclaimed your life."

He reached out and slid one hand over the heavy fall of her hair and arched a brow. "What's next?"

She'd rehearsed what she wanted to say. She'd written it down, polished it and memorized it as if it were a part in a play. She'd figured it'd give her control over the discussion.

But her mind was blank.

"I love you," she said.

"I love you, too."

Their kiss was gentle and sweet, making Sophia's heart sing and her toes tingle. Slowly, Max pulled back to look into her eyes.

"I didn't want to love you," he confessed. "I wanted to be able to walk away. Hopefully set the memory of you aside so you weren't in my way."

Her brows shot up. He grimaced.

"Not like that." He paused, trying to find the words. "All my life, I've felt penned in by rules. My family's rules. Uncle Sam's rules. Hell, even my own rules. I accept them all, and understand their value. But sometimes I just have to break one. Like seeing you. I knew you could make me break my number one rule, but being with you was worth the risk. But a part of me was afraid you'd put strings on me and do what my uncle failed to—make me take the easy career path and end my respect for what I was doing."

He stopped, watching her face. Sophia couldn't believe his fears were the exact same ones she had herself. Different, but the same.

"I'd never want to hold you back," she said softly.

"I know. I finally realized that. You pushed me to confront my uncle, to fight for my station. You cared enough about what mattered to me to let me pursue it."

"Like I said," she told him, "I love you."

His smile flashed just before he took her mouth. His lips seduced, sweet and sexy as they moved softly over hers. He pulled her closer, so her breasts pressed against the stiff fabric of his jacket. His medals poked her shoulder, adding an oddly erotic element to the kiss. Sophia melted into him. Their tongues slid together in a familiar dance of passion.

"I want to marry you," he said quietly, drawing back just enough to look into her eyes.

Sophia's heart raced. Oh, yes, she wanted to yell. She wanted to dance around the garden and clap and laugh with joy. But she couldn't.

"I can't marry you," she said quietly, holding tight to his hands so he wouldn't step away.

He frowned and shifted. Not away, but enough so that they were no longer plastered together.

"Is it because my mother vandalized your gallery and tried to ruin your business?" he asked. Sophia had to smile at the grim resignation in his tone because beneath it she heard the exasperated love.

"Of course not. I actually understand why she did it. And she's more than made up for any problems she caused by hosting the series of Friends of Esprit Gallery luncheons. Who knew high society was so interested in naked breasts?"

Max's smile flashed, but just as quickly it was gone.

"Then the fact that she'd posed with her naked breasts isn't the problem?"

She had to give him credit. He barely cringed as he said the words. She figured it was his military training. The man faced live bombs; he wasn't about to back away from his mama's wild past.

"No. Like I said, I understand why she tried to hide it, but I also understand what it's like to be seduced into letting go of all inhibitions."

"Right," he muttered, obviously more comfortable with his mother having her inhibitions intact. Then he shrugged it off, obviously not wanting it in his brain. "If it's none of that, then what is it?"

Sophia licked her lips, sitting on the edge of the fountain and trying to gather her nerve.

"Here's the thing," she started.

Max shook his head.

"Nope. I don't want to hear about the thing," he insisted. But he was smiling.

"The thing is, I love you."

He reached out to pull her into his arms, but Sophia shook her head.

"I love you. But I'm not ready to take that step. I'm afraid."

"Of marrying a soldier?"

"No," she insisted, jumping to her feet then and pressing her palms against his chest in assurance. "Oh, no. You were a soldier when I fell in love with you. I know your job is scary. It's dangerous and hellish and it means you're away for long periods of time. But I knew that when I fell in love with you."

"Then what's the problem?"

Sophia sucked in a deep breath. "I'm afraid of losing myself. You're a strong man. You know what you want. You've got a plan and you know where your life is going."

Max frowned, shaking his head in confusion. "So? You're a strong woman. You've got a gallery and you know what you want for it, right?"

"Yes. But it's not enough." She looked over his shoulder at the adobe estate, still amazed that she had her home back. Not because she'd suddenly gotten brave, but because Max had pushed her off the cliff. "I need to figure out where my life is going. Once I know, I can share it with you."

"Does this involve other men?"

"No!" she exclaimed, horrified.

"Then go for it."

She laughed. "Just like that?"

"Sure. I want you to be happy. I can't think of anything you'd do that I couldn't support."

She took a deep breath, then blurted, "I want to be a photographer."

"Are you planning an exposé of men's anatomy?" he asked.

"Eww."

"Then, again, why wouldn't I support you? You're a fabulous photographer from what I've seen. Whatever you need, just tell me. You want me to do security at your shows, I'm there. You want me to drive you to remote mountains so you can take shots of wildflowers, just say so. You want me to do nothing and stay out of it, I'll try my best. This is your dream, sweetheart. You're calling the shots."

She didn't know what to say. She couldn't think of a single reason. So she hugged him instead.

Not for the support, although that was amazing. But because he hadn't even blinked at the concept of her being a photographer. He'd met famous ones. He'd been a part of a quarter-million-dollar exhibit this past weekend. And he believed in her so much that he didn't question that she'd fit all of that.

It made her brave enough to continue.

"I want to be with you," she told him. "I want to give us a chance. But like you said, I need to do this on my own. I need to know I'm strong enough to marry you."

She held her breath. She'd taken more risks in the past week than she'd taken in her entire life. But this one scared her the most.

"I want to travel and take pictures," she admitted. "There's so much I want to see and do. So much I want to learn about myself. I'd visit you if you'd let me, but I don't want to promise anything until we're both sure."

Max was silent at first. Sophia's stomach tilted toward her toes. He puffed out a breath, then leaned his forehead on hers and closed his eyes. Then he pulled back and gave her a look of such intense love, her eyes stung. No, she wasn't going to get all emotional here. She was going to stay in control.

"You need this time?" he said. "Then take it. I'm in the war zone for a year. I'm sure I'll be stationed stateside after, unless you'd rather I request something else."

"You're willing to wait for me?" she asked, knowing tears were leaking down her cheeks but unable to stop crying. At least she'd learned from Tabby to wear waterproof mascara.

"Sweetheart," he said, lifting both her hands to his mouth and pressing a kiss on her knuckles, "I'd be waiting anyway. I'll do it better if I know you're happy until I get back."

Epilogue

Two years later

"ARE YOU SURE THIS ISN'T too cliché?" Sophia asked, her voice shaky with nerves. "It's like Saint Valentine went crazy."

Silver hearts and red roses. Chocolate and champagne. Love and romance. It was almost too perfect.

Tabby smoothed her hand over the heavy white satin of Sophia's skirt with a giddy sort of smile. The kind inspired by a proud mother or a woman who'd already downed half a magnum of champagne. Or in this case, both.

"It's perfect," the older woman declared. "You're perfect. In that dress. For this day. And most of all, for my Maximilian."

My Maximilian, Sophia silently corrected.

Who knew they'd actually make such a crazy relationship work, let alone work so well it'd flourish into a three-tiered cake and flower girl?

Max had completed his tour overseas with Sophia flying off to some exotic locales to meet him for a few days here, a week there. They'd written. They'd talked on the phone. They'd discovered that the rush of lust and excitement that'd launched their relationship was solid and lasting and real.

And today, they would promise to spend the rest of their lives together.

She'd risked it all. And she'd gotten everything she ever dreamed of in return. Both in love and in her career. While she traveled, Tabby and Gina ran the gallery, which was a surprisingly perfect pairing. On a roll with her success, Sophia had nagged von Schilling into mentoring her. It'd taken her a year to get past her insecurities. But Max had been there for her, totally believing in her. Then last month, her shots of the women in Afghanistan had won an award.

Sophia stepped into the hallway and took her father's arm. His kiss on her cheek, the music and cheers as she walked down the aisle were all a distant blur.

There were hearts and flowers decorating the garden and she knew Rico was standing as best man. But all she saw was Max, there in his black tuxedo, waiting for her at the altar.

In her mind's eye, she snapped a picture of this moment. Of their future together. She wouldn't need to analyze it, though.

She knew it was going to be amazing.

* * * * *

COMING NEXT MONTH

Available February 22, 2011

REQUEST YOUR FREE BOOKS!
2 FREE NOVELS PLUS 2 FREE GIFTS!

Harlequin *Blaze*

red-hot reads!

USA TODAY *bestselling author Lynne Graham*
is back with a thrilling new trilogy
SECRETLY PREGNANT, CONVENIENTLY WED

Three heroines must marry alpha males to keep
their dreams…but Alejandro, Angelo and Cesario
are not about to be tamed!

Book 1—JEMIMA'S SECRET
Available March 2011 from Harlequin Presents®.

JEMIMA yanked open a drawer in the sideboard to find Alfie's birth certificate. Her son was her husband's child. It was a question of telling the truth whether she liked it or not. She extended the certificate to Alejandro.

"This has to be nonsense," Alejandro asserted.

"Well, if you can find some other way of explaining how I managed to give birth by that date and Alfie not be yours, I'd like to hear it," Jemima challenged.

Alejandro glanced up, golden eyes bright as blades and as dangerous. "All this proves is that you must still have been pregnant when you walked out on our marriage. It does not automatically follow that the child is mine."

"'I know it doesn't suit you to hear this news now and I really didn't want to tell you. But I can't lie to you about it. Someday Alfie may want to look you up and get acquainted."

"If what you have just told me is the truth, if that little boy does prove to be mine, it was vindictive and extremely selfish of you to leave me in ignorance!"

Jemima paled. "When I left you, I had no idea that I was still pregnant."

"Two years is a long period of time, yet you made no attempt to inform me that I might be a father. I will want DNA tests to confirm your claim before I make any decision about what I want to do."

"Do as you like," she told him curtly. "*I* know who Alfie's father is and there has never been any doubt of his identity."

"I will make arrangements for the tests to be carried out and I will see you again when the result is available," Alejandro drawled with lashings of dark Spanish masculine reserve.

"I'll contact a solicitor and start the divorce," Jemima proffered in turn.

Alejandro's eyes narrowed in a piercing scrutiny that made her uncomfortable. "It would be foolish to do anything before we have that DNA result."

"I disagree," Jemima flashed back. "I should have applied for a divorce the minute I left you!"

Alejandro quirked an ebony brow. "And why didn't you?"

Jemima dealt him a fulminating glance but said nothing, merely moving past him to open her front door in a blunt invitation for him to leave.

"I'll be in touch," he delivered on the doorstep.

What is Alejandro's next move? Perhaps rekindling their marriage is the only solution! But will Jemima agree?

*Find out in Lynne Graham's
exciting new romance
JEMIMA'S SECRET*

*Available March 2011
from Harlequin Presents®.*

Start your Best Body today with these top 3 nutrition tips!

1. **SHOP THE PERIMETER OF THE GROCERY STORE:** The good stuff—fruits, veggies, lean proteins and dairy—always line the outer edges of the store. When you veer into the center aisles, you enter the temptation zone, where the unhealthy foods live.

2. **WATCH PORTION SIZES:** Most portion sizes in restaurants are nearly twice the size of a true serving and at home, it's easy to "clean your plate." Use these easy serving guidelines:
   * Protein: the palm of your hand
   * Grains or Fruit: a cup of your hand
   * Veggies: the palm of two open hands

3. **USE THE RAINBOW RULE FOR PRODUCE:** Your produce drawers should be filled with every color of fruits and vegetables. The greater the variety, the more vitamins and other nutrients you add to your diet.

Find these and many more helpful tips in

YOUR BEST BODY NOW
by
TOSCA RENO
WITH STACY BAKER

Bestselling Author of
THE EAT-CLEAN DIET®

Available wherever books are sold!

NTRSERIESFEB

ROMANTIC SUSPENSE

Sparked by Danger, Fueled by Passion.

CARLA CASSIDY

Special Agent's Surrender

There's a killer on the loose in Black Rock,
and former FBI agent Jacob Grayson isn't about
to let Layla West become the next victim.

While she's hiding at the family ranch under Jacob's
protection, the desire between them burns hot.
But when the investigation turns personal,
their love and Layla's life are put on the line,
and the stakes have never been higher.

A brand-new tale of the

LAWMEN *of* BLACK ROCK

Available in March wherever books are sold!

Visit Silhouette Books at www.eHarlequin.com

SRS27718

HARLEQUIN *Presents*

USA TODAY *Bestselling Author*

Lynne Graham

is back with her most exciting trilogy yet!

SECRETLY PREGNANT CONVENIENTLY WED

Jemima, Flora and Jess aren't looking for love,
but all have babies very much in mind...and they may
just get their wish and more with the wealthiest, most
handsome and impossibly arrogant men in Europe!

Coming March 2011
JEMIMA'S SECRET

Alejandro Navarro Vasquez has long desired vengeance after
his wife, Jemima, betrayed him. When he discovers the
whereabouts of his runaway wife—and that she has a two-
year-old son—Alejandro is determined to settle the score....

FLORA'S DEFIANCE (April 2011)
JESS'S PROMISE (May 2011)

Available exclusively from Harlequin Presents.

HPI 2975